Freely Written

Vol. 1

Susan Quilty

Cover Design: Susan Quilty
Publisher: Bitter Lily Books, LLC

ISBN: 978-1-7379702-8-6
ISBN: 978-1-7379702-9-3

Bitter Lily Books, LLC
Ashburn, Virginia

SusanQuilty.com

Included stories previously appeared on the Freely Written podcast, hosted by Susan Quilty.

The Stories

Grocery Store Sushi
Membership
A Drop in the Ocean
Take a Seat
A Stitch in Time
The Cat's Pajamas
The Passage of Time
Spaghetti and Meatballs
Muffin of the Month
Squirrelly
Parking Lot Friends
The Goose in the House
Writer's Block
Duck à l'Orange
Unicorns and Rainbows
Fireside Wine Chat
Rain or Shine
Pumpkin Spice
Storage War
A New Leaf

An Introduction

Welcome to *Freely Written, Vol. 1*, a collection of short stories curated from the *Freely Written* podcast.

If you haven't listened to the podcast, it's based on a simple premise of sharing stories that were free-written from writing prompts, with no planning and very little editing. Each story is about 10 minutes long and may be written in any style.

Freely Written is hosted by me, Susan Quilty. I write all of the stories, though I am happy to accept suggestions for future writing prompts—and give you credit if your prompt is chosen. A simple word or common phrase can spark many interesting ideas, and I never know where a free-written story will go!

You may be wondering why some of the stories have been collected in this book, when anyone can listen to them on *Freely Written* for free. Great question!

Creating this collection wasn't my idea. It's a suggestion I've gotten from a few listeners, and I decided it's a good one. While podcasts are great, I still prefer to curl up with a book, and I love short books I can toss in a bag and read whenever I have a quick break.

After reading this book, maybe you'll find your way to my podcast or decide to check out my other books.

This may be a good time to explain that my writing process for *Freely Written* is very different than my approach to writing novels.

While my podcast may suggest otherwise, I'm a writer who relies on deep research, careful planning, and copious editing. My extensive outlines span multiple spreadsheets, and I've spent countless hours cross-checking everything from subway schedules to scientific speculation on the climate of a planet orbiting two suns to be sure my fictional worlds are grounded in reality.

That may be why I created *Freely Written*.

With all the careful crafting I put into my novels, I also need time to let my imagination run free. Free-writing snippets of fiction has been a creative outlet for as long as I can remember. Some of those snippets have made their way into my books, but most are left scattered through the notebooks that gather dust on a lower corner of my bookshelf.

When I joined Patreon (Patreon.com/SusanQuilty), I began sharing some of my unplanned and unedited free-writing with my patrons. Some of those stories had a second life as the earliest episodes of *Freely Written*, and three (*Grocery Store Sushi, Membership,* and *The Passage of Time*) are also included in this book.

I was initially nervous about sharing such raw, unpolished writing, but I soon found there can be joy in sharing so freely.

Of course, writing fiction with no planning or editing can have mixed results.

Sometimes, I'm pleasantly surprised with the finished story. Sometimes, I'm not. Usually, I can find something I like about it, even if it didn't quite hit the mark.

This is one of those experiences where the journey may be more valuable than the destination—though I have done my best to include the more satisfying stories in this collection.

Only you can be the judge of which stories you like. As a writer, I offer words that I hope have value. As readers, you interpret that value for yourself.

§

After each story in this collection, you will find its *Freely Written* episode number and air date. You can use that information to listen to the story on *Freely Written*, either through your favorite podcast app or at FreelyWritten. buzzsprout.com.

You will also find a brief note about each story. If you want more commentary on a story, or on my writing process, you can find bonus commentary episodes on the *Freely Written* podcast.

For the most part, stories in this book are listed in the order they aired. There are some exceptions.

On occasion, I've revisited characters in multiple *Freely Written* episodes. That happens in two groups of stories in this book. While each of these stories stands on its own, they've been published back-to-back here.

The first set includes three stories: *The Goose in the House, Writer's Block,* and *Duck à l'Orange.*

The second set includes two stories: *Unicorns and Rainbows,* and *Fireside Wine Chat.*

You may also notice that this collection is marked as volume 1. If your favorite *Freely Written* story didn't show up in this book, let me know if you'd like to see it included in volume 2.

You can contact me through my social media accounts or message me at susan@susanquilty.com. Remember, you can also send me suggestions for future writing prompts.

As I said earlier, listening to my podcast is free. However, creating and hosting it is not. Purchasing this book helps offset those costs, and your support is greatly appreciated!

On to the stories...

Grocery Store Sushi

It was going as well as Catherine had expected. She hadn't wanted to meet Craig for coffee. She hadn't wanted to meet Craig at all. But Miriam had pushed, and here they were, sipping lattes at an outdoor café in the chill of early spring.

"Get out more!" Miriam had said. "You've been alone too long."

And Catherine had agreed with that. She just hadn't been keen on the blind date idea. Especially when Craig's strongest selling points were that he smiled a lot and always turned in his weekly reports on time.

"Okay, so I don't know him well," Miriam had admitted. "But he seems nice enough around the office, and it's just coffee. It's not like you have to marry him!"

After meeting him, Catherine made a mental note to tell Miriam that Craig's constant smiling was not a selling point. Also, that he'd immediately taken to calling her Kate, even after she'd clearly introduced herself as Catherine.

"Do you eat grocery store sushi, Kate?"

"What?" Catherine looked at Craig across the rim of her cup, feeling sure her wandering mind had missed some relevant context.

"Sushi," he repeated, flashing the smile that was more smarm than charm. "From a grocery store. Do you eat it?"

Catherine hesitated, unsure if he was making conversation or suggesting lunch plans.

"A lot of people say they won't touch it," Craig continued confidently. "They say they only eat sushi from a restaurant. But every grocery store around here sells sushi, so you know a lot of people are eating it. Right?"

"I guess." Catherine tried to sip her coffee but found it was still too hot.

"I eat grocery store sushi," Craig added, nodding smugly at his own confession. "I really like it, too."

"Uh huh," Catherine muttered, her attention shifting toward an oddly dark cloud in the otherwise clear blue sky.

"Of course, it's not the same as fresh sushi from a good sushi bar, but it can be pretty close, depending on where you get it."

"Uh huh." Catherine was barely listening. The cloud was growing larger and other people had noticed it as well. Some pointed to the sky. Others intently scanned their phones.

"Now, I draw the line at gas station sushi," Craig clarified. "If there isn't someone there, making it on site, I don't buy it. But most grocery stores around here have someone making it fresh. That's the difference for me."

"Yeah, um, Craig?" Catherine broke in, gesturing toward the sky. "I think something is happening."

"Huh." Craig turned to casually examine the dark cloud, which was looking less cloud-like by the moment. "That's strange."

"Yes…" Catherine paused, bothered by his apparent lack of concern. She fished her phone out of her bag and unlocked it with her thumb.

Craig turned his back on the dark object.

"You can tell a lot about a person by the sushi they eat."

"What?" Catherine looked up in confusion.

"You know, like if they only eat California rolls and avoid raw fish," Craig explained, still sporting his perpetual smile. "Or if they won't admit to liking sushi from a grocery store."

"Uh huh."

Catherine's news app filled the screen with reports of mysterious dark objects that had been spotted over several major cities. As she scanned an article, people hurried out of nearby businesses to stare up at the sky. Many pointed their phones toward the dark object, taking pictures or talking over live video streams. Others typed rapidly or held their phones to one ear.

"It takes a bit of trial and error."

"What?"

Catherine was standing now, feeling the fervor of the moment and barely aware of Craig's continued presence.

"To find which places have good sushi," he answered, now standing by her side.

"Uh, yeah, Craig…" Catherine began awkwardly, then decided to be direct. "This isn't the time to talk about sushi."

Crowds were forming along the sidewalk. Passing drivers stopped their cars, causing a traffic jam of blaring horns. A few drivers got out to yell. One tried a three-point turn, leading to a screech of brakes from a car in the opposite lane.

People in the crowds nudged each other, urgently sharing whatever updates they had found on their phones. Someone loudly asked, "What do we do? What do we do?" to no one in particular. A toddler cried loudly, and two women knelt on the sidewalk to openly pray.

"They say to go indoors!"

The message was passed from somewhere in the center of the crowd. It carried no specification of which "they" had given the order but sounded official enough to get people moving.

Catherine barely had time to grab her handbag before she was swept into the coffee shop amid a surge of jostling strangers. When the movement settled, and the double doors were closed, she turned to see Craig beside her, holding both of their coffee cups.

"Thanks," she muttered, taking her own cup and surveying the scene. About twenty people stood in the café's small seating area. Employees who had been outside now retreated behind the barrier of the coffee bar.

It was oddly quiet as the strangers assessed each other, coming to grips with the potential enormity of their situation. Eyes darted and feet shuffled.

"Does anyone have a signal?" A worried voice called out. "I lost my connection."

Murmurs of concern grew as each person confirmed they could no longer access the news with their phones. An employee said he'd check the WiFi. Someone told him that didn't matter. Arguments broke out over why there was no internet connection and what they could or couldn't do to fix it.

"Hey!"

Catherine startled as Craig stepped toward the center of the room. He still gripped his coffee cup but was no longer smiling. Instead, he wore a confident air that immediately silenced the crowd.

"Something strange is going on out there," he acknowledged, "and we don't know what it is. We're all a little scared, but panicking isn't going to help anyone."

Mumbled assents filtered through the crowd, while many nodded their agreement.

"Until we have more information, we should take a moment to settle in and pull ourselves together. Agreed?"

Catherine smiled softly, realizing her first impression of Craig may have been too critical. He had calmed the crowd with ease and was now directing everyone to pull up chairs so they could sit together in a large circle. Shyly, she made her way toward him and felt a surge of pride when he smiled at her and patted the empty seat beside him.

Once they were all comfortably seated, the group turned toward Craig as their natural leader. He took a sip of his coffee and straightened his shoulders, enjoying the attention.

Catherine saw the gleam in his eye and her smile froze. He wouldn't, she thought in a horrified flash. But he did.

With a self-satisfied grin, Craig raised one hand and asked, "Who here likes grocery store sushi?"

§

Grocery Store Sushi - Ep. 1, March 16, 2021

While this is the first story I shared on *Freely Written*, it was originally written for my Patreon page (Patreon.com/ SusanQuilty). The phrase "grocery store sushi" makes me smile, and I may find another use for it in the future. Maybe as a fictional band name.

Membership

"Hello?"

"Hello! Do I have the pleasure of speaking to Mrs. Almina Solak?"

The cheery voice rang from the receiver with a force that pierced Mina's ear. Hastily turning down the volume, she answered with a wary, "This is Almina Solak."

"Oh, Mrs. Solak, it's so nice to speak to you!" The voice was high-pitched, though likely male. Mina racked her memory for an identity to match its somewhat familiar sound but came up empty. "May I call you Almina?" The voice continued. "Or would you prefer Mrs. Solak?"

"Uh, Mina," she muttered, realizing that the voice belonged to a stranger. Another telemarketer. "I go by Mina."

"Mina it is!" The voice was entirely too happy about this decision.

"Uh, who is this?"

Mina pursed her lips and looked out the back window. There was snow covering the ground and the driveway looked icy.

"Oh, my, yes! I should have begun with that," the voice sang lightly. "My name is Chip and I'm calling from the Part of This World Foundation."

"Part of…" Mina had only half-listened after Chip shared his name. She was preoccupied with calculating the odds that this bright voice actually belonged to a man named Chip or if it was part of the persona he used to sell whatever it was he was selling.

"Part of This World," Chip repeated with the same upbeat lilt.

"I, uh…" Mina waited for him to continue his spiel, but the line stayed patiently silent.

Mina heard a car start and moved to the front of her small house. Frank Hoffman was scraping the ice off his windshield while clouds of steam billowed out of his tailpipe. *He would be one to go out in this mess,* Mina thought to herself. Frank was always going somewhere.

"Did you say, *part of this world?*" Mina asked after shaking herself out of her wandering thoughts and realizing she still held the phone in her hand.

"Yes, ma'am," Chip answered brightly. "The Part of This World Foundation."

Mina turned from the chilly front window and walked back into the kitchen where her electric tea kettle had begun to boil. *This is nonsense,* she thought, while opening a tea bag to place in her favorite mug, but she was intrigued by Chip's silence.

Most telemarketers rushed on without pause, barely letting her get in word, as if sure that word would be *no.* Which it usually was, she conceded, but she often thought she wouldn't mind hearing them out before making up her mind, if only they weren't so pushy about it. And, now, here was Chip with his cheery voice and polite pauses, giving her plenty of time to gather her thoughts and respond in her own time.

"Well, all right then, tell me about this foundation of yours," Mina prompted grudgingly as she leaned back against the counter. She might as well listen while she waited for her tea to steep.

"Oh," Chip sounded surprised. "You aren't familiar with the Part of This World Foundation, I see…"

This pause had a different weight and Mina stood up taller.

"Should I be?"

This is ridiculous, she scoffed at the defensive clench in her chest. *Just another new sales tactic.*

"I'm checking your membership records now…" Chip tapped away at a keyboard with loudly clacking keys. "Ah, yes," he answered with the sound of a smile. "I see, now. Your husband had managed your account before…" His voice faltered, and Mina felt her lips tighten.

"My husband…?" Her voice was tight. This was not the first call that had tried this angle, though she somehow hadn't expected it from Chip.

"It appears your husband, Daniel Solak, had assumed your account ownership directly from your mother, which may tell us why you are not familiar with the foundation." His explanation sounded both reassuring and vaguely concerned, though he quickly put his worries aside.

"It's fine!" He went on. "I'm happy to walk you through the options… it's just been a while since I've come across a dormant account where the owner hasn't been… Well… that doesn't matter now, does it?"

"I, uh…"

Mina was having trouble following Chip's meaning, but she felt better when he swept his momentary conflict away and returned to his bubbly, confident tone.

"Previously, you had a joint membership account at the Bronze level. That's four to seven close friends each, three dozen acquaintances, the Fitness Lite package, a choice of three community interests, and two volunteer opportunities—No, wait, you had the volunteer upgrade with, oh my, five volunteer opportunities. That *is* a kind way to spend your social credits! The Bronze level also includes up to two pets, though it seems you haven't exercised that option in a few years now. No children, but unlimited bandwidth for friends' children."

Mina sat on a kitchen chair; her tea was forgotten on the counter.

This is a joke, she thought as she watched the snow that had begun to fall. *This is a prank, a farce, a scam, a…*

"Mina?" Chip's voice was a bit softer. "Are you still there?"

"What?" Mina blinked the room back into focus. "Yes, I'm here. But this… This is…"

"You had been registered at the Bronze level for quite a while," Chip continued, "about 23 years, it seems. With the change in your circumstances, you'll want to consider your other options now."

Mina stood up to fetch her teacup. *I should hang up,* she told herself.

But she didn't.

"Your individual membership account at the Bronze level would be similar, with some adjustments. However, many in your situation find that this is a good time to try an upgrade. At least for the first year or so. An upgrade to the Silver level would let you maintain your current friendships and activities, while also allowing space for meeting new people and trying out new interests. Then, after some time, you can always reassess and go back to the Bronze level… adjusting for the elements you'd like to keep going forward.

"Although…" he sounded thoughtful, "you've let your Bronze level account lapse for several months now, so if you'd rather resume at that level—ease yourself back in— you can always upgrade at a later date."

Mina pulled her phone from her ear and stared at it with a deep frown. She let her arm go slack and paced around her small living room with her phone dangling by her side. The house was exactly as it had always been, though perhaps a bit dimmer and dustier. It had been some time since she'd had anyone over. Friends had left casseroles and groceries at her door for weeks, but she couldn't remember the last she'd received. Her freezer and pantry were gradually emptying without being replenished.

She hadn't left the house much either. There were solitary walks in the early hours or after dusk, timed to avoid neighbors. There were a few errands, though Mina couldn't remember the last place she'd gone. She hadn't felt up to book club, or babysitting at the women's shelter, or helping at the food pantry. She hadn't been to the gym in months.

Mina stopped in front of the fireplace, studying her wedding picture on the mantel, then quickly lifted the phone back to her ear.

"Chip?" She sounded afraid. "Are you still there?"

"Yes, Mina," Chip replied pleasantly. "I'm still here."

Mina took a deep breath and felt tears stinging the corners of her eyes.

"I don't quite understand all this," she admitted with a crack in her voice.

"It can be overwhelming," Chip agreed gently, "but I'm happy to go over all of your options in more detail."

"Not just the options…" Mina trailed off. She didn't understand any of it. How it had come about. When it had fallen apart.

"I'll explain all of it," Chip reassured. "We can start at the beginning and go from there. Step by step."

"This is all new to me," Mina whispered, glancing around as if someone would hear.

"Yes," Chip agreed softly, "but it isn't too late to learn."

Mina smiled. She was glad she'd answered the phone.

Membership - Ep. 2, March 23, 2021

This story was first written for my Patreon page (Patreon. com/SusanQuilty). The writing prompt came from spying the word "membership" printed across a donation-gift notepad. That's likely why I began the story with a call from a telemarketer. I created The Part of This World Foundation as I typed and love the concept that unfolded.

A Drop in the Ocean

Carol kicked the dirt below her swing, watching dusty particles float up into the sky. Her chin bowed toward her chest and her hands gripped the metal chains. She could hear Nana approaching but didn't bother to look up.

There was a creak of old metal and a crackle of stiff joints as the neighboring swing took Nana's weight. A soft sigh followed, and then it was quiet.

Some adults would ask outright if they wanted to know what was wrong with a child, but Nana wasn't that kind of adult. She simply sat in the swing beside her granddaughter and watched the clouds of dirt that appeared with each kick.

Carol watched some tiny bits of dirt float away, wondering how far they would get before gravity pulled them back to the ground. She liked to think that she was setting them free and sending them on adventures. But what if they only made it a few feet away and were stranded in the lush grass with nothing to show for it?

She stopped kicking the dirt and looked up at the trees. There was a woodpecker nearby. She could hear it but hadn't caught sight of it. Birds made Carol think of flying above the treetops, soaring high in the sky.

"Nothing I do matters," she said suddenly, surprising herself with the words.

Nana rocked lightly in her swing, waiting to see if Carol had more to say.

"I try and try, and no one even notices," Carol went on. There was a tremble in her voice, followed by a catch that suggested she wasn't finished.

"Jemma sold the most cookies again, and this time she won a new bike."

"And you want a new bike?" Nana asked softly.

"No." Carol shook her head. "Mine is fine. It's not the bike, it's the…" She searched for the right words to finish her sentence.

"The winning?" Nana suggested.

Carol kicked up another cloud of dirt.

"I don't know. Maybe."

She weighed her answer, decided it didn't feel right, and scrunched her brow as she tried again. "No, I don't care that she won exactly. Sabrina broke her arm, and I don't want to do that."

"But you feel the same way about Sabrina as you do about Jemma?"

"Huh." Carol shrugged. "Sort of, I guess."

"A little jealous?" Nana asked, using a tone that said it was okay.

"Uh… maybe," Carol admitted reluctantly. "But I don't want what they have. I just want…"

She trailed off again, feeling her way to the answer.

"To be noticed?" Nana guessed, finally drawing Carol's full attention.

When their eyes met, Carol felt her chest swell and her heart pick up its pace.

"Mama's raising money for another charity." It sounded like Carol was changing the subject, but they both knew she wasn't. "For some kind of cancer, I think."

Carol's mother worked for an organization that raised a lot of money for a lot of different charities. She was always putting on social events and pledge drives.

"One of the moms at school gave her a check for $150," Carol confided. "It was at pick-up, and once the lady left, I said it must be great to get a check like that. But Mama said it was just a drop in the ocean, like what that lady gave didn't really matter at all."

"That made you angry?" Nana asked, noticing the rise in Carol's voice.

"Well, yeah, kinda," Carol admitted. "Mama said she gets checks for ten times that amount all the time. I mean, she did add that it was nice of the lady to make a donation. But she said it like she didn't really think it meant that much."

"I see," Nana sighed.

Carol looked at her grandmother, feeling her eyes go wide with the effort of trying to explain.

"I'm like that check," she said, her voice hoarse with strain. "I'm like that drop in the ocean that doesn't really matter. Nothing good I do stands out to anyone."

Other adults might have criticized Carol's mother then, saying that she should be equally grateful for every donation no matter how big or small.

Maybe they would say that $150 might not be a lot of money for a wealthy business owner but it was a lot of money to most people.

Nana was not that kind of adult.

"You want to be a drop that leaves the ocean?" she asked gently. "A drop that does something more interesting than float with the other drops."

Carol's eyes lit up and her mouth began to twitch into a smile.

"Like the water cycle," she said haltingly, still working out her idea. "We learned about that in school. Water evaporates up in the air to make clouds and travels all around before splashing back down as rain."

She beamed for only a moment before a new thought darkened her face.

"But it's not like the whole ocean gets to evaporate. It's probably just the special drops. The rest of them probably have to stay in the ocean and watch while the others get to make clouds and rainbows."

Nana leaned back in her swing, making the metal frame creak as she gripped the chains and looked up at the sky.

"Why not?"

Carol looked at her grandmother in confusion.

"Why can't every drop in the ocean evaporate?" Nana clarified. "Sure, the ocean is big, but look at all those clouds! And they're very vary away. Imagine how big they'd be if we were right up there with them."

Carol cocked her head skeptically.

"Look!" Nana pointed. "There's a plane flying right in front of that little cloud. See how small the plane looks from here? Now, think about how big a plane is when it's on the ground."

"Oh, yeah," Carol breathed, watching the plane glide past. "That cloud is so much bigger."

"And it's one of the smallest clouds up there today," Nana added. "And the clouds are constantly moving and changing, which takes a lot of water. So, I think there's a good chance all the drops in the ocean make it up there eventually. Even if they don't always know when it will be their turn to fly."

Carol thought about that, smiling softly to herself.

With a sharp creak of metal, Nana pulled back and launched her swing into motion. Her legs kicked forward as her back reclined. With each pass, she bent and straightened her legs, creating a wider and higher arc. Carol laughed to see Nana's long hair sweep the ground and to hear her hollers of joy.

"Come on, Carol," Nana called. "Come fly with me!"

Setting everything else aside, Carol launched her swing into motion, letting each arc take her closer to the cloudy blue sky.

§

A Drop in the Ocean - Ep. 3, March 30, 2021

The sweet innocence of this story sets it apart from the more quirky stories I often free-write. It's the first story I wrote specifically for *Freely Written* and continues to be one of my most popular.

Take a Seat

Sunlight bathed the forest, though little light made its way through the lush foliage to the winding turns of the hidden stone path. The stones in this path were old, cracked by shoots of green and half-covered by encroaching ferns.

In some places, thin saplings divided the stones, leaving Hayden little room to pass without feeling the snag of brambles that had created an arching tunnel over the trail of stone. But Hayden was persistent.

He did not know what he would find at the end of this stone path, but he believed it would be worth the journey. Just as he had believed he would find the path when others had insisted it was a myth.

"I have a map!" Hayden had declared boldly, waving the scroll above his head.

"A map you made!" Was the typical retort, as his friends laughed and ordered more ale.

"It's still a map," Hayden had insisted, though with a softer tone.

He knew the work that had gone into his map. The hours of research, the interviews with village elders, and the careful plotting against the landmarks of a starry sky. After weeks, he'd found the right patch of forest, though his friends had refused to believe.

"There's nothing in that wild place," his cousin Merle had said. "Not if you leave the Golden Road. Just twisted vines and branches and brambles, too thick to house a thing."

"But it was there," Hayden had asserted quietly. "Long before the Golden Road cut a swath through the forest. Before Moorvale connected through to Langshire. Before Moorvale was even a proper village. There was the old stone road that led to the soul's desire."

"Bah," Merle had scoffed with a dismissive toss of his shaggy head. "Legends and nonsense."

"But the poems…" Hayden had pleaded. "The songs… There can't be so many references to something that doesn't exist."

Merle had not been convinced, and neither were any of their friends. And so, Hayden had set out on his own one dewy morning with nothing but a small pack of provisions and hope in his heart.

Before the sun was fully overhead, Hayden had glimpsed the tunnel of brambles that were said to shield the remains of the stone path. He'd already been quite deep into the forest by that point and had collected signs of his toil. There were fine scratches on his face and hands, small rips in his shirt and pants, and bits of twig stuck in his braided hair.

He'd been tired, but his discovery had spurred him forward, giving him the strength to hack his way through the thinnest bit of spiky branches and stagger out onto the unmistakable remains of an old stone road.

Now, as the hours passed and his steps grew weary, Hayden began to wonder why he'd ever come on this journey at all. What had made him so intent on finding his soul's desire? What could that even mean? And how would he know if he'd found it?

As he walked, deep in shadows, he noticed a beam of sunlight streaming across an upcoming bend in the path. He'd seen similar rays break through the brambles from time to time, but nothing as wide and promising. His feet itched to run, but Hayden willed his legs to keep their steady pace. He did not want the hope in his heart to burn too bright, for fear of it being extinguished by too large a disappointment.

Yet when he reached the bend in the path, there was no mistaking the source of the light. As the crumbling stones turned to the left, they opened onto a small clearing draped in lavender and alive with the flight of blue butterflies.

A smile broke across Hayden's tired face. He dropped his pack at the edge of the clearing and lightly stepped forward to bask in the sunlight. As his long arms extended, Hayden closed his eyes and turned in a grateful circle.

A soft laugh startled his movement. Hayden's arms fell by his side and his head whipped toward the sound, freezing at the sight of a young woman with light coppery hair and a dress made of gauzy white linen.

"Welcome," she greeted graciously, her voice like warm honey.

She settled herself on the soft grass, letting her dress billow and rest around her. Two dragonflies hovered near her left shoulder and she offered them a friendly smile before they flitted away.

"Take a seat," she invited, gesturing to the grass before her.

Hayden hesitated, unprepared for this discovery. The elders had spoken of finding his soul's desire, yet none could say what that would be, and none had suggested there would be a beautiful woman waiting to bestow it.

"Come," the woman encouraged. "It isn't difficult to take a seat."

Her words surprised Hayden, though he knew she was right. He'd sat down plenty of times in his life. At home, in the fields, at the tavern. Never in a mystical clearing with an enchanting woman, though he supposed the act of sitting was still the same.

Hayden settled to the ground across from the woman, taking care to leave a respectful distance while still being close enough to speak comfortably. He could not see her legs beneath her flowing dress, though she appeared to be sitting with her knees bent and shins crossed before her. Hayden assumed the same seat.

"Close your eyes," the woman invited, lowering her own eyelids.

With her eyes closed and her shoulders relaxed, the woman appeared entirely at ease in the forest clearing. Hayden was less content but forced his eyes to close. His face squinched with the effort and his shoulders tightened around his ears. The sounds of the forest grew louder, every rustle and chirp caused Hayden to flinch, but he was determined to keep his eyes shut.

This is it! He thought eagerly. *I'm about to get my soul's desire.* He wondered if he should turn up his palms or hold out his hands, but no further instruction came. After seconds that felt like hours, Hayden cracked one eye open to see the woman still sitting serenely before him. Though her eyes were closed, she smirked lightly.

"You do not have to close your eyes," she offered, keeping her own closed. "You can simply soften your gaze."

Hayden let his eyes stay open, unsure what it meant to have a soft gaze. His entire body felt tense and hard, shaking from an effort to control his expectations. The woman stayed silent, simply breathing deeply in the late afternoon sun.

After a moment, Hayden tried to follow her example. He took a deep breath in and let it out with a trembling shudder. He took another breath, telling himself to be patient. After his third breath, his shoulders began to relax and still the woman was silent.

"Excuse me," Hayden ventured softly.

The woman opened her eyes, still lightly smiling.

"I, uh, I was told that this is the place where I would… uh, find my soul's desire."

"Yes," the woman agreed pleasantly.

"Well, uh…" Hayden did not want to seem impatient.

"You have found it," the woman assured him, though her words had the opposite effect.

"This?" Hayden looked around in disbelief. "This is it? Finding this clearing?"

A worrisome thought occurred to Hayden.

"Am I to stay here forever now?" He thought of the long journey through the woods, the scratches of the brambles, and the exhaustion of his endless trek. "Have I died?"

"Died?" The woman laughed merrily. "Oh, no, my friend. You are quite alive, and you will return to your village. But you will take a piece of this clearing with you."

Hayden looked around again, eyeing the lavender and passing butterflies. They were lovely, but not unique to this clearing. If he brought them back, his friends would say he'd only collected them from the meadow.

"I don't understand," Hayden admitted.

"You will," the woman assured gently. "For now, it's enough to take a seat and simply breathe."

Hayden blinked rapidly, unsure of her words but feeling an unfamiliar glow in his chest. It wasn't the hope in his heart, but something deeper.

He yielded with a sigh, closing his eyes, and feeling the warmth of the sun on his face. His shoulders softened. His jaw relaxed. And, for the moment, Hayden's soul was at peace.

§

Take a Seat - Ep. 7, April 20, 2021

This story was inspired by my friend and fellow yoga teacher, Gretchen Schutte. Meditation can sound intimidating to new students, so Gretchen simply calls it "taking a seat." Anyone can take a seat. Add a focal point (such as mindful breathing or a repeated mantra) and you're meditating. You can practice meditation and yoga with Gretchen through PeaceinthePause.com.

A Stitch in Time

The old woman sat beside her grown daughter, a length of black velvet draped across her lap and a golden needle flashing between her deft fingers. This velvet fabric was unlike any other fabric in the realm. It had been woven by elves in the ancient Minilamian Wood, presented to Queen Nateur II, and passed down through 27 generations of Karahnaray royalty.

Its rich ebony was sprinkled through with the finest touch of diamond dust, creating a sheen that reflected light in muted glimmers. When one observed the fabric from a distance, it appeared to have a subtle pattern of swirls and eddies. Deep blue on dark black with elusive greens and pinks that only appeared when the fabric was turned slowly against a direct light.

Yet, this darkness was a deception.

When one sat close enough to pass the fabric beneath his or her hands, images emerged from the field of mottled, shimmering darkness. On first pass, these images were bright orbs. Some stitched in vibrant blues or greens. Others textured with rustic reds, oranges, or yellows. Many orbs were adorned with a cluster of small adjacent dots of color, while some were bisected by finely stitched rings.

Those lucky enough to closely examine this legendary fabric responded with giddy delight during their first encounter. For as the fabric passed through their hands, the images shifted before their very eyes. As one selected an object, say a yellow-striped orb that had been the size of a thumbnail, it would grow with each turn of the fabric, expanding until it filled the visible surface, revealing intricate textures woven by mystical fingers. As one continued to turn the cloth, the image of whichever orb had been selected might shift into closer focus still, revealing a landscape of dusty rock, frozen lakes, or wind-swept terrain.

By far, the favorite orbs were those that expanded to reveal hidden civilizations. Clusters of tiny creatures posed against various natural or created structures, interacting with each other, or depicting fascinating scenes.

Depending on the position of the fabric, careful turning of the cloth might reveal a scattering of families frolicking on a sunny beach, a lone adventurer scaling a rugged mountain, or a crowd of people and strange vehicles milling past towers of metal and glass.

There were endless wonders within the cloth. Those who were most adept in its handling could uncover cozy scenes of lovers settled before glowing hearths, lovely babes asleep in their cribs, or exotic animals hunting prey through endless savannahs. Stories were written and songs were sung about the charming, romantic, or frightening scenes found by those skilled at turning the cloth.

Just as the ownership of this magnificent fabric had been passed down through generations of royalty, so too had its care been passed down through a family of tapestry-skilled mystics. The old woman had begun to learn the secrets of the cloth when she was a small child and, in time, had passed the secrets of her skills to her own daughter.

Today, they would focus their attention on a much-loved, blue-and-green orb. As this was a favorite attraction of the royal family, the hidden scenes within this particular orb were prone to additional wear.

"Shall we begin with a seaside town or the complications of a city?" the daughter asked her mother, gently draping the fabric across her lap and balancing her own needle in the crook of two fingers.

"Ah, I would love a visit to the sea," the old woman sighed, "though there are many cities that are more in need of our attention."

Mending the magic cloth was an arduous endeavor, half-skill and half-intuition. The miniscule scenes never emerged the same way twice, yet over time, people and objects began to take on a ragged appearance. As these forms began to show signs of tatters, the scenes they depicted became gradually more tragic. Conversely, those with well-tended forms were apt to display scenes of joy and celebration.

Generally, the royal family and their distinguished guests were amused by both the tragic and celebratory scenes. In fact, some in the current family preferred the drama of the darker imagery and would implore the weavers to let some portions of fabric fall into disrepair, simply to see what emotional scenes may play out on future viewings.

This was a difficult request for the weavers. The family line charged with the care of the cloth had great compassion for all of the creatures within its mystical folds. The old woman in particular was loath to leave a single creature, structure, or natural element without prompt mending. Yet the care the cloth required was considerable and the old woman could not keep up with it as well as she would like. Simply seeking out which areas to mend was time-consuming, particularly as her energy and eyesight had begun to fade.

"When will your Edyth be joining our work?" the old woman asked her daughter pointedly.

"Mama," the daughter sighed, "Edyth is far too young to hold a needle let alone begin to sew."

"Hmmph," the old woman grunted. She was cross that her daughter had waited so long to have a daughter of her own. When she had been a girl new to the cloth, she had stitched beside her mother, grandmother, and great-grandmother.

"You were not so young when you had me," the daughter chided, sensing the turn in her mother's thoughts.

"That was not by choice," the old woman rejoined, shutting out the painful memory of the daughters she had not been blessed to bear.

"I know, Mama," the daughter replied softly, chastened into silence.

Yet she did not have to speak for the oft-repeated argument to echo between them.

Times were changing, the daughter had said on many occasions. Women did not have babes so young anymore, and those coming into the world now were less inclined to carry on with family obligations that had been sworn before they were ever born.

It was an appalling thought to the old woman. The idea that the tapestry-magic of her family—the honor of mending the great royal fabric—might not be a welcome continuation through future generations.

Truth be told, she was less concerned with the waning tradition of her family line and more heartsick at the thought of the tiny woven creatures that were going without timely care.

"They are only bits of thread and silk," the daughter reminded absently.

"Yes, yes, I know," the old woman agreed, quickly wiping a tear from her weathered cheek.

"You work too hard," the daughter persisted. "You stay up mending into the night. You miss meals. You work your fingers to the bone. And for what? The amusement of the royal family and their honored guests?"

The old woman tensed at her daughter's impertinent words.

"It is not for the royal family that I work so hard," she responded stiffly.

The daughter sighed, looking at the scene they had uncovered in a densely populated city within the fabric. The buildings were frayed, the sky was washed out, and the tiny people were hunched in misery. She disliked these tragic scenes and preferred to let them fall to pieces as she stitched on scenic pastures or shaded forests.

The old woman held her needle above the fabric, her hand shaking as she considered where to begin today's work. There was so much to be mended and she was only one woman.

§

A Stitch in Time - Ep. 11, May 11, 2021

Sitting with this prompt, my mind instantly pictured an old woman stitching on a magic cloth. Though I didn't know what magic it held, zooming into the details of the cloth led me to uncover its secrets. I love to imagine this brief scene as part of a larger fantasy novel.

The Cat's Pajamas

The lion was not pleased. As usual, the cat was regaling the pride with an epic tale of his adventures with the humans. And, as usual, the entire pride—from the youngest cubs to the oldest lions—were held in rapt attention. Everyone, that is, except the lion who had first discovered the cat watching him from a high branch on a spindly tree.

The lion had been intrigued by the cat's unflappable cool. Despite her tiny size, she'd leisurely lounged on the thin branch, craning her neck to eye him critically. Her languid gaze had suggested boredom, yet the lion had been keen enough to catch a gleam of calculation in her pale blue eyes.

Beyond the strangeness of her being in the tree at all, the cat's appearance was made even more perplexing by the flowered pink garment she wore over her cream-colored fur.

"What are you doing up there?" the lion had asked, cocking his enormous head to one side.

"Oh, not much," the cat had called down, swishing her tail against the branch beneath her.

"What are you?" the lion had tried again, thinking it best to begin at the beginning.

"I'm a cat," the cat had sighed, rolling over to sit more primly on her perch.

Cat. The word had tumbled through the lion's mind searching for a meaning. In his world, the term cat referred to all lions and to his many cousins of varying lineages. The leopards, the tigers, the cheetahs. But he'd never come across a cousin that was as tiny as this strange creature.

"What kind of cat?" the lion had asked after a long pause.

The cat had sighed, licking her paw and smoothing the pale fur between her dark ears.

"Siamese," she answered in time, though the lion had sensed there was more to this answer.

"And you live around here?" He'd asked, still assessing this strange discovery.

"Not exactly," the cat had responded, standing up to stretch her back with a languorous shake.

"What does that mean?"

The lion had begun to lose patience with this small creature. He'd been fairly sure she wasn't a threat but had not yet decided if she might make a nice meal.

"Well…" The cat had resettled on the branch, keeping a careful distance from the lion. "I'm not from here originally. I traveled to the area with my humans but was separated before they decamped."

"Humans!"

The lion had experienced enough of the humans to know that they were a threat to him and his pride. He had circled the tree then, looking in every direction for signs of the danger.

"They aren't here," the cat had reassured, before yawning leisurely. "I told you, they decamped. They're long gone, probably on their way to Egypt or China by now. They are quite the travelers, my humans."

"Your humans?" The lion had settled uneasily beneath the cat, studying the pink cloth she wore over her fur. It certainly seemed like the kind of cloths he'd seen the humans wear over their bodies, though softer perhaps.

"Yes," the cat had shrugged then with just a touch of sadness. "They were my pets, and they were good to me. I will miss them now that they are gone."

"Your pets?" the lion's head had begun to hurt. "What are pets?"

"Oh, dear," the cat had sat up straighter, injecting her words with an air of pity. "You've never had a pet? Well… pets are creatures that you keep for companionship. They bring you food, entertain you, and generally do your bidding. My humans also took me around the world on magnificent adventures. It was quite a nice relationship."

The lion had taken that in slowly, considering what it might be like to have pets to do his bidding. As the leader of his pack, he was revered by his pride and feared by their prey. Yet, he'd never had another species bring him food or strive to entertain him.

Certainly not the humans who came in with their fearful weapons that could fell a lion with a sudden explosive force. He'd been impressed by the idea of a creature that could master such powerful predators, especially one so small and unassuming.

"You're alone then?" the lion had asked, noticing a gleam in the cat's eye. "Would you like to spend some time with my pride?"

And that was how the tiny cat had become part of the lions' daily life.

There were some ground rules to be set before the cat was introduced, and the lion was careful to impress that the cat was under his protection. Yet, it hadn't taken long for the rest of the pride to accept the cat without that admonition.

They enjoyed the cat's colorful stories and were enchanted by her swift motions as she darted throughout the grasslands. Her pink cloth—pajamas as she called them—were another source of both amusement and admiration. Amusement because it was strange to see an animal in human clothing and admiration because it signaled her mastery of the humans.

While the rest of the pride grew to adore the cat, the lion began to begrudge her place among them. The cat did not hunt with the other lions. She did not provide food for the pride, and she was certainly incapable of being a mate to even the smallest lion.

She distracted the cubs from their lessons and the older lions from their work. Though she was never distinctly rude, she made often light of his leadership, teasing him to lighten up and have more fun.

Worst of all, she had won the pride's hearts in a way the lion had not.

The lion was not pleased by her presence and wanted to show it in some small way. His opportunity came when he happened upon the cat's pajamas stretched on a rock by the watering hole.

The cat, wearing nothing over her fur, was fishing a few feet away and looked even smaller without the pink fabric swathed around her body.

The lion patted the pink fabric, feeling its dampness and seeing the trails of water that trickled off the rock. The sun was high overhead and no one else was about.

"The trouble with pajamas," the cat called over casually, "is that they need to be washed from time to time. And it's so much nicer to let them dry in the sun before putting them on again."

"Ah," the lion replied, not entirely understanding but grasping that the cat's pajamas were unprotected as she focused on catching a fish.

Without her pajamas, the cat seemed to lose some of her magical air. She also blended into their surroundings more easily, which could make her safer… or could make her more easily mistaken for their natural prey.

It would only take a quick swat of his paw, the lion realized. He could push the pajamas into the watering hole and let them float away before the cat returned. Losing her pajamas might not take away her stories or her charm, but it was one thing the lion could take away and he wanted to take something from her.

The lion raised his paw, about to push the pink pajamas into the water, when a shot rang out in the distance. Birds flew up from a nearby tree and the ground shook with a rumble of approaching doom. The lion had felt that rumble before and knew it preceded the arrival of humans in wheeled vehicles with explosive weapons.

"Run!" the cat shouted, forgetting all about the fish that had been in her sights.

The lion took off across the dry grass, bounding away from the danger, before a nagging worry brought him to a halt. He spun around to see the cat still at the water's edge, squirming her body into the damp pajamas.

"What are you doing?" The lion roared, leaping back to her side. "You have to run!"

"No, you have to run," the cat hissed, shoving her front paws through two of the pajama legs. "I have to get dressed. I have to show them where I belong."

"But…" the lion studied the cat in confusion. "You belong with the pride."

The cat looked up at him, her tiny face still in the shade of his shaggy head.

"You don't want me in your pride," she told him plainly. "I don't hunt for food and I can't mate to expand the pride. I don't have anything to offer you."

The lion shook his head, seeing the humans' vehicles rumbling into the distance.

"That doesn't matter," he insisted wildly.

"You teach us about the humans, you entertain us, you… you… Well, I don't know. But we like having you around."

The cat sat back on her haunches, considering her options carefully, as if they were not on the verge of being attacked by a human hunting party.

"You want me around?" she asked in disbelief. "Truly?"

The lion glanced at the approaching vehicles, seeing an explosive weapon being raised toward their position.

"Yes, yes, you silly cat!" he cried in fear.

"Well, okay, then."

The cat leaped onto the lion's back, climbing high enough to grip his unruly mane.

"Now, run!" she yelled, and he did, carrying them back to their waiting pride.

§

The Cat's Pajamas - Ep. 13, May 25, 2021

Idioms make great writing prompts, especially when they're as cool as "the cat's pajamas." If I were planning out a story, this may have taken a different direction. With free-writing, I let my subconscious take over instead. The first sentence —*The lion was not pleased.* —drifted into my mind and I followed it into the savanna.

The Passage of Time

Aoife stared down the corridor in awe. Its walls swirled with eddies of blues and green, dashed through with splashes of violet and mauve. The ground was a polished white stone that gently reflected the light from those glowing blue-green walls. And the ceiling…

Aoife's breath caught as she lifted her eyes to the canopy of stars above.

As her eyes darted across the sky, she took in clusters of shining stars—galaxies of light—that varied in subtle shades of pearl, diamond, and gold. Behind those stars, the sky was inky blue in places and pale pink in others. Colors that meandered together in shifting rivulets, feathering into each other in soft, reaching tendrils.

Shaking her head, Aoife pulled her mind back from the magnetic draw of this stunning corridor. She blinked three times, then closed her eyes. After a deep breath, she fluttered her eyes open, pleased—and concerned—to see that this strange hall of color and light was still here. Still stretching into the depths of what had been—only moments before—her rather cluttered kitchen pantry.

Still gripping the edge of the pantry door, Aoife considered simply closing the mystical closet and going on with her day.

But that didn't seem like a very good option.

The hall of light was gaping before her, and her plans for baking a three-layer cake would have to be put on hold. Particularly because the flour, sugar, and vanilla had all disappeared into this unfathomable improbability.

When Sasha joined Aoife in the kitchen, she cut right to the point.

"What did you do?"

"Me?"

Aoife glanced her way, afraid to turn her attention from the corridor for long. "I didn't do anything. I opened the pantry to get the flour and it was like… this."

"Flour?" Sasha turned to her friend with a pleased grin. "Were you making me a cake?"

"What?"

Aoife, who had been mesmerized by a shooting star, needed a moment to make sense of her friend's question.

"Well, yes," she confirmed at last. "It's your birthday, and I was making you a cake."

"That's so sweet," Sasha sighed. "I love your baking. Were you making a vanilla cake?"

"With strawberry frosting," Aoife agreed distractedly.

"That's lovely," Sasha smiled, then frowned at the glowing hallway. "Shame you weren't able to make it."

"I'll make one later," Aoife promised. "But, uh, first can we focus on the, uh, shining, swirling, hallway to…"

She trailed off, the icy truth of the situation washing over her.

"Where is it a hallway to?" Aoife whispered shakily.

They stared down the corridor soberly. Beyond the shimmering walls and dazzling sky, it was hard to see anything else. The far end of the corridor was shadowed and too distant to have discernable details. What slight movements they could see could be from the swirling lights or from shifting, unnamed creatures. It was impossible to tell.

"Have you tried stepping inside?"

"What? No!" Aoife was startled by the suggestion and perplexed to realize that she hadn't even considered such a thing.

Aoife's stomach trembled as she watched Sasha extend her arm over the pantry threshold.

"What does it feel like?" she whispered in awe.

"Nothing," Sasha answered with a hint of disappointment.

Her arm was bathed in blue-green light but otherwise seemed unaffected. She lifted one foot, preparing to step into the corridor, when Aoife gripped her arm in fear.

"What are you doing?"

Aoife could hear her heartbeat thundering in her ears, but Sasha only shrugged.

"Seeing where it leads," Sasha shrugged nonchalantly. "Are you coming?"

Aoife turned back toward the kitchen. She let her gaze drift over the familiar surroundings lovingly, wondering if she would ever see them again. Her mixing bowls and baking supplies were on the center island. The wall oven's display showed that it had been successfully pre-heated long ago. The coffee pot was filled and ready to brew at the touch of a button, as she'd been getting ready for Sasha's birthday visit.

"I don't know…" she hedged, turning back to face the glowing hall.

"Well, I do," Sasha responded saucily. "And it's my birthday, so you're coming with me. That can be my present, since you didn't bake my cake."

"Your cake…" Aoife muttered. She'd been thinking about Sasha's cake when she'd opened the pantry. Not just thinking about it but worrying about it. Worrying about having enough time to bake and frost it before Sasha arrived. There never seemed to be enough time.

"On the count of three," Sasha commanded, firmly taking Aoife's hand. "One… two…"

On her count of three, they both stepped forward, crossing the threshold into the otherworldly glow of the fantastic corridor. As they did, their wonder fell away. The walls ceased to hold their attention. The starry sky lifted away. There was no temperature in the space. No sensation in the space. It was a space that simply existed and in it, Aoife and Sasha also simply existed.

Without care. Without conscious thought.

Sometime later, in what could have been a blink of the eye or a full calendar year, Aoife and Sasha found themselves sitting at Aoife's cozy kitchen island. The vanilla cake with strawberry icing sat on the island beside a steaming pot of coffee and two ceramic mugs.

"You baked me a cake," Sasha observed, pleased but strangely uneasy.

"Of course," Aoife smiled, feeling similarly unsettled. "It's your birthday."

"Where do you find the time?" Sasha grinned, swiping a bit of icing with her fingertip.

"Oh, I don't know," Aoife laughed, setting aside the odd sensation of having no concrete memory of baking this cake. "I just go about my day like anyone else."

"Well, I appreciate it," Sasha beamed, hiding her unease at not remembering the last half of her drive to Aoife's house. "There's no one I'd rather spend my birthday with!"

"Make a wish!" Aoife cried, delighted at how the day had turned out.

§

The Passage of Time - Ep. 16, June 8, 2021

This story was first written for my Patreon page (Patreon. com/SusanQuilty) and was inspired by the calendar changing from 2020 to 2021. What a strange year!

Spaghetti and Meatballs

Jeff pushed a half-full cart down the brightly lit aisle while Tiffany skimmed her digital shopping list. The grocery store was quiet this time of day. Jeff liked having the store mostly to themselves, and he liked hearing songs from his teen years playing over the loudspeakers.

"Did we decide what to make for dinner tomorrow night? When Cindy and Rick come over?"

Tiffany checked an item off her list and shrugged.

"No, but let's keep it simple."

"Oh, of course," Jeff agreed. "I was thinking spaghetti and meatballs would be good. The meatballs can simmer while we visit over drinks, then we just need to throw in the spaghetti when we're ready to eat."

"Hmm," Tiffany hesitated.

She knew Jeff was excited for this visit and didn't want to squelch his enthusiasm.

"Is there something wrong with spaghetti and meatballs?"

Jeff pushed the cart around a fallen box of cereal, then bent to put it back in its proper place. Their daughter couldn't come to town very often and on this trip, she was finally bringing her boyfriend to meet them. Jeff thought some hearty comfort food would make the right impression.

"Well, kind of…" Tiffany began gently.

"Oh, right," Jeff jumped in. "I know you can't have wheat anymore, but we can do a pot of rice noodles for you and regular pasta for the rest of us. You like rice noodles with meatballs and sauce, right?"

"I do," Tiffany agreed. "But Cindy and Rick are vegan."

"They're what?" Jeff stopped the cart and looked at his wife in confusion. "Since when is Cindy vegan? She had a hamburger at our Fourth of July party."

"She had a veggie burger," Tiffany corrected. "Black bean and tofu. She made it inside while you were at the grill."

"Oh." Jeff didn't know what to say. His daughter was an adult and could eat what she liked, but it felt strange to not know she'd given up meat.

"Okay, well, we can pick up some veggie meatballs, right? I mean, they must make them if they make veggie burgers."

"Yes…" Tiffany agreed carefully. "But I can't eat soy, so I'll just have plain sauce on my noodles."

"Oh, right," Jeff frowned.

"Well, I'm not exactly excited about trying the meatless ones myself, so we'll make both. Meatless meatballs for the kids and meat meatballs for us. Huh… that sounds weird."

They laughed over his choice of words and made their way down the aisle.

"So, two pots of sauce with different types of meatballs, and two pots of water for the different noodles?"

"Sure, why not!" Jeff laughed, happy to have solved her worries so easily. "We have four burners, might as well use them."

"I guess we can make a salad to go with it," Tiffany offered. "I'll add spinach to the list."

"Let's have a caprese salad instead," Jeff countered as they turned the corner at the end of the aisle. "Get some fresh mozzarella, and we'll use tomatoes and basil from the garden."

He could picture impressing Cindy and Rick with a beautiful platter of layered tomatoes, basil, and cheese dressed with a drizzle of olive oil and a sprinkle of fresh cracked pepper.

"Uh, Jeff," Tiffany reminded, "They're vegan. No mozzarella. No cheese."

"But cheese isn't meat!" Jeff blurted out, louder than intended, then hurried on as another couple turned their way.

"Vegan means they don't eat any animal products. So not just meat, but also cheese, eggs, butter…"

"Butter?" Jeff stopped again, his face falling. "How do I make my signature garlic bread without butter?"

Tiffany shrugged.

Having not eaten wheat in years, she couldn't quite grasp Jeff's love of bread at every meal.

"Olive oil?" She suggested, turning to examine the rows of jarred olives.

"Yeah, maybe…" Jeff's grand plans for a traditional family dinner were beginning to feel complicated. "They do eat olives, right?"

"Yes, of course," Tiffany smiled. "We can set some out to snack on before dinner."

"Yeah, okay," Jeff brightened. "Maybe with some arti-chokes and roasted red peppers?"

"Sure," Tiffany agreed. "And some crackers for the rest of you."

Tiffany tapped at her digital list while Jeff pictured the four of them nibbling at a colorful tray of pre-dinner snacks while the stove bubbled away with two pots of sauce and two pots of noodles…

"Maybe this is a bad idea," Jeff worried, gripping the cart handle as Tiffany gently placed jars of olives in the cart.

"What is?" Tiffany was alarmed to see the color had drained from Jeff's face.

"We're making two dinners…" He stammered ner-vously. "One for us and one for them. What kind of message is that? That isn't a welcome to the family dinner! That's a dinner designed to point out their differences…"

Jeff's voice rose as his tone became mocking, "Hi, Rick, nice to meet you. Your dinner is over there and ours is over here. You don't really belong. And, sorry, honey, you don't belong anymore either. You're with Rick now. Go have your dinner from that side of the stove!"

"Jeff, breathe!" Tiffany stepped close, rubbing her hand over her husband's back and making her own breaths slow and steady. "That's it, in and out, just breathe."

After a few shaky breaths, Jeff felt steadier. He peeled his fingers from the cart handle and noticed the dampness of his palms.

"She's never brought a boy home to meet us before," he told Tiffany timidly. "Not since high school."

"I know," Tiffany soothed, still rubbing her palm in circles on his back.

"I want to make a good impression," Jeff admitted, beginning to feel a little foolish about his outburst. "Maybe we should just forget cooking and order pizza."

"Without cheese?" Tiffany asked, a hint of a smile creeping over her face.

"What?" Jeff looked confused, then shook his head with a laugh.

"Because they're vegan," he and Tiffany said together.

Jeff glanced around the store, hoping no one had witnessed his minor meltdown and smiled at Tiffany sheepishly.

She smiled back, saying, "They will love the spaghetti and meatless meatballs."

§

Spaghetti and Meatballs - Ep. 23, July 20, 2021

Growing up, I was the only person I knew who had food allergies. There's more awareness around food-related health issues now, but the limitations can still be hard for others to understand. I love Jeff's compassion in planning this family dinner.

Muffin of the Month

"Hello, is this Derek Evanson?"

Derek shifted in his seat, hesitating to confirm his identity to the stranger on the other end of the line. She sounded pleasant enough but calling from a private number felt vaguely suspicious.

"Who's calling?" Derek asked in what he hoped was a casual, friendly tone.

"Is this Derek Evanson?" the woman repeated, sounded mildly concerned. "Maybe I have the wrong number, I can be so flustered sometimes."

Her nervous laugh reminded Derek of the blonde he'd met in the park last week. The blonde who'd cautiously accepted his business card after he'd struck up a conversation about dog groomers.

"No, you have the right number," Derek responded with a smile. "This is Derek."

He pictured the woman's long blonde hair and tried to remember her name. *Sarah? Suzie? Samantha?* An admin walked past his open office door, and he tried not to seem too pleased with himself as he leaned back in his leather chair. First the promotion, now the pleasant surprise of this call.

"Oh, good," the woman sighed with relief. "We've been trying to catch you for some time."

His smile faded as Derek sat upright.

"We keep missing you," the woman continued breezily. "It's always your voicemail, and I guess you've been too busy to call back."

"I, uh… Who did you say you are?"

Derek felt his knee knock against the underside of his desk, and he willed his leg to stay still.

"Oh, my, I don't think I did say, did I?" the woman laughed, sending a prickling heat across Derek's clenched jaw. "I'm Peg, from the Muffin a Month Club."

Jumping up from his desk, Derek shut his office door. Two junior salesmen looked over at his closed door before shrugging and getting back to their conversation. Now hidden from their view, Derek leaned against the door and took a deep breath.

"I cancelled your service two months ago," Derek snapped into the phone. "Or I tried to, but your… *Muffins* keep showing up, and I keep sending them back, and you keep billing me."

"Actually, we haven't been able to bill your since you closed your credit card," Peg informed him patiently. "I'm calling about getting an updated card."

"An updated card?" Derek squawked with a sound that was somewhere between a laugh and a snort. "I'm not giving you an updated card!"

"But, sir, you do have a contract with us," Peg reminded him kindly.

"But I cancelled," Derek persisted. "I cancelled two months ago."

"Yes," Peg agreed politely, "but your contract calls for a three-month commitment before cancelling."

"And I waited three months before canceling, and two months before closing that credit card, so you already have five months payment." Derek shook his head, upset at himself for ever subscribing at all.

"But you never accepted delivery of any of our Muffins." Peg sounded perplexed. "Your commitment wasn't just for the money, but for three months of Muffins."

"Well, that's absurd!" Derek slouched against the door, then pulled himself up to pace toward his desk. "You have my money, and I received nothing in return. That should be more than enough to satisfy my contract!"

"I see," Peg sighed.

Derek could hear rapid typing over the phone. He simultaneously wondered what she was typing and why her keyboard was so loud. Both questions competed for attention, beginning to give him a headache.

"I'm afraid that's not what you agreed to in your contract," Peg told him gently. "Our Muffin of the Month Club is quite clear in its contracts, and it does require accepting at least one Muffin."

"But you didn't send Muffins!" Derek blurted in agitation. "They were..." he trailed off, unsure how to finish the sentence without sounding like a jerk.

"I beg to differ," Peg returned primly. "The companions brought to you each month were all named Muffin."

"Yeah, but..."

Derek sat behind his desk, feeling the flush spreading across his cheeks. The narrow window beside his office door looked out on a maze of cubicles and all the employees who worked for him. What would they think if they knew what kind of club he'd joined one late, lonely night.

"But...?" Peg prompted, forcing him to spell it out for her.

"Muffin is a *cute* name," Derek began weakly. "And the pictures on your site are all young and cute, but what you sent me... They were some of the most... well the most *uncute*... unlovable... dogs I've ever seen."

"I see."

Peg's stiff answer brought a fresh flush to Derek's face. He could feel the nervous sweat breaking out under his arms and across his upper lip.

"That does seem like a rather snap judgment, considering you never accepted delivery on any of the companions brought to you..."

"Oh, come, on!" Derek groaned in annoyance. "Did you see the dogs they sent me?"

There was a pause as Derek became aware of how loud he was speaking. He glanced out the window nervously and made a mental note to lower his voice.

As Peg sat in silent judgement, Derek quickly typed in the club's website. His screen was filled with images of fluffy puppies frolicking on grassy lawns or curled up in cozy laps. A video began to play, and Derek quickly muted it.

On his screen, a handsome man in a stylish suit held a docile puppy in each arm. He smiled, nuzzling each dog, as the closed captioning displayed his words:

Do you want the love of a puppy without the long-term commitment? Our Muffin of the Month Club is here to help. Each month, we can bring you a new puppy to love—all named Muffin for ease of memory. Enjoy time at the park, take long walks, teach your Muffin new tricks, and at the end of each month, you can turn your Muffin in for a new model. Pause your subscription anytime or cancel after three months. No questions asked.

"Sir? Sir?"

Peg's prodding broke through Derek's reverie.

"Yeah," he mumbled, still watching the adorable puppies playing on his screen.

"Once you've updated your card, you can receive delivery of your next Muffin."

"What? No," Derek sputtered. "I don't want any more of your Muffins. The dog's you sent me were ragged and gaunt. One had a lame back leg, and one never stopped growling. The first one wasn't so bad, I guess…"

Derek's memory ran through each dog that had been brought to his door, stopping on the spindly mutt with an impossibly frizzy face. "But it was…" he stopped short of saying *ugly.*

"Our Muffins are *rescues,*" Peg stressed, "and you were told there would be no guarantee on breed. Now, if you'll just give me your new card number…"

"I can't have another dog," Derek insisted with a shake of his head.

"Another dog, but…?" Peg hesitated. "Our service is only for people without other pets."

"Yeah, well… I didn't have a dog when I signed up," Derek admitted reluctantly. "But after seeing your, uh, companions, I decided to pick out my own puppy."

"I see," Peg responded frostily.

Derek felt his anger rising, pushing aside the shame she seemed intent on provoking.

"Look, the only mistake I made up was signing up for your stupid subscription in the first place. What kind of place let's people turn in a puppy for a new model every month? What you're doing is sick! And, yeah, you can look down on me for getting a cute puppy from a breeder, but I'm actually committing to my pet. I'm the good pet owner here!"

Derek finished in a rush, taking a few rapid breaths to calm his outburst.

"Sending our dogs out for one-month trials keeps them out of shelters," Peg said softly.

"What?" Derek blinked.

"They're fostered while we look for forever homes, though people who take them for one month often fall in love and end up adopting. The Muffin a Month Club is just a gimmick to get attention… Did you even read your contract?"

"Oh, uh, I…" Derek stumbled. He vaguely remembered hearing something about that when he called to apply for the program, but he'd been really busy then, hustling for his promotion and hadn't really been listening.

"It's okay, sir," Peg told him quietly. "I'll cancel your contract."

"Oh, uh, okay." Derek felt a mix of emotions he couldn't name. "Thanks."

After he hung up the phone, Derek looked at the picture on his lock screen. The sight of his precious corgi's adorable face with its white muzzle and bright eyes brought a lightness to his heart.

Though he suddenly felt strange about naming her Muffin.

§

Muffin of the Month - Ep. 24, July 27, 2021

The beauty of free-writing is that it can lead in unexpected directions. Sometimes, when I think a story might be too predictable, I challenge myself with a twist. This story has several twists, mainly for my own amusement.

Squirrelly

"Order! Come to order!" Chelsey Sylvain called sternly, cutting through the chatter that had taken over the meeting.

Those nearest quickly fell quiet, while those in the back continued to chitter on, albeit more softly. Chelsey shook with agitation and bared her teeth in a controlled grimace.

"I said, ORDER!" She barked with enough force to silence the assembly.

"That's more like it," she muttered, before quickly launching into her agenda. "Now, we have a serious matter to discuss. It's one that's come up before as a side matter, but I'm afraid the situation is becoming dire."

A few attendees smirked or nodded knowingly. Others looked uncomfortable as they twisted their forepaws or shook out their bristling fur. One in the back wrapped his tail around his body, stroking its bushy fur in mindless worry.

"Yes," Chelsey continued, rising higher on her powerful back legs. "We have observed a steady increase in what can only be called humanly behavior, and it must stop!"

Beside her, the council barked and trilled in approval, yet concerned chattering had again broken out through the gathering. Many in attendance felt that the council was too narrow in deciding which behaviors were acceptably squirrelly and which fell into the humanly realm.

"We have observed many excursions into human neighborhoods, which are, of course, perfectly acceptable hunting grounds. However, there are codes of conduct that are being disregarded.

"For example, foraging seeds from feeder contraptions is a time-honored squirrel tradition. Yet, participating in human-made games to reach the rewards of seeds or nuts is a demeaning activity which has been forbidden by this council. Some of you continue to flagrantly disregard that ban to the point of behaving more like trained creatures of a circus than proud woodland denizen."

A trio of squirrels in the center of the room stiffened as several eyes glanced their way. It was true. The Atwood siblings—Margo, Reginald, and Clive—had found a human home where elaborate structures led them through perilous obstacles with increasing rewards of their favorite seeds and nuts.

They knew participating in such human games was considered un-squirrelly by the council, but they felt proud of their ingenuity in securing a steady food source. The others glancing their way waited to see if Margo, Reginald, or Clive would finally stand up to the council on this controversial matter.

Yet they stayed silent, and Chelsey shifted her attention to others in attendance.

"And I am not only talking about the most flamboyant among you," she clarified pointedly. "I'm referring to all squirrels who have the temerity to ingratiate themselves with a single human family."

Attention shifted from the Atwood siblings as many squirrels looked down nervously. It might be against the council's wishes, but for common squirrels, befriending a human who was willing to set out daily rations was well worth putting on a bit of a show or giving the humans the thrill of eating from their sweaty palms.

"Point of order!" An old gray squirrel called from the back of the group.

Chelsey sighed with a soft whistle, drooping her upper body slightly before rising back to her full two-footed height.

"The chair recognizes Nolan Hayward."

Nolan rose on his haunches, pleased to have the floor though hiding it under an officious air.

"The French Fry Doctrine allows for the procurement of food through human interaction when other food sources are scarce."

Several squirrels nodded agreement, though their support was more about the tastiness of human food—French fries in particular—than about the civic debate of acceptable squirrelliness.

"Yes," Chelsey conceded stiffly.

She had long been an opponent of the French Fry Doctrine, saying that it would never pass with today's council, and occasionally trying to have the rule repealed. However, that was unlikely to happen, as even the strictest member of the squirrel council enjoyed the salty treat of a stray French fry.

"Yet even in the French Fry Doctrine, distance from humans is preferred when procuring human food. That should apply to all food varieties, even a natural diet of nuts and seeds.

"Furthermore," she said loudly, breaking through another wave of subdued chatter. "We are seeing many of you opting for these human-given foods even when acorns are plentiful!"

"Acorns!" Nolan scoffed as he settled back to all fours. A murmur of scorn rippled through the gathering, causing an aggravated chattering among the council.

It was true that acorns were plentiful in their oak forest. And it was true that the squirrels loved to bury acorns to eat in the winter. But many squirrels were not content to live on acorns alone. Especially when humans were willing to provide so many other options.

"We have a responsibility to tradition!" Chelsey barked, shaking her bushy tail in consternation.

More than half of the squirrels nodded agreement. They couldn't say why, but they felt that responsibility deep in their bones. Gathering and burying acorns, pinecones, berries, and other delicacies was not an activity that any were willing to give up.

Yet many also felt that it no longer mattered if the source of those delicacies were from pilfering trees and the forest floor or from taking the offerings of generous humans. Most would be buried for winter anyway… except for French fries, of course.

"Perhaps…" A small voice squeaked from the front of the gathering. Its high-pitch timidity caught the notice of the crowd, and the gathering grew quiet.

Chelsey turned impatiently, then softened at the sight of her small son—Chester Sylvain—balancing on two feet and holding a forepaw in the air for attention.

"Perhaps," he began again. "We should have less rules about what defines squirrelly behavior."

Chattering echoed this sentiment until Chelsey held up both forepaws for silence.

"We must have rules," she told her son patiently, "to continue our squirrel heritage. Without rules where would we be? Why, I've even observed some young squirrels playing with sticks like an ordinary dog!"

Gasps and whistles from the crowd nearly deterred Chester, but he bravely stood his ground.

"But isn't independence the most squirrelly behavior of all?" He asked earnestly. "And isn't squirrelly behavior any behavior carried out by a squirrel?"

All eyes turned to Chelsey. She stood mute, frozen in place, before gradually sitting back on her haunches.

Subdued grunts from the council suggested they were also ruffled by this suggestion, but Chelsey scarcely took note of them.

She looked at her small son and thought, *Is a squirrel more squirrelly when it's left to its own independence? What does it mean to be squirrelly?"*

After a moment of reflection, Chelsey shook herself to attention and glanced at the judgmental eyes of the council.

"I propose further discussion among the council and a review of procedures at our next gathering," she decided firmly. "Meeting adjourned!"

The squirrels darted into the forest, happily chattering away. Some set out in search of French fries, others chased friends around nearby tree trunks, and the Atwood siblings set out to see what their humans had set out for them today.

§

Squirelly - Ep. 27, August 10, 2021

This prompt was suggested by my oldest and best friend, Wendy McMullan. She sent it with a video of a squirrel she saw playing with sticks in the park. It was adorable and funny, and great inspiration for a story!

Parking Lot Friends

On Mondays, class let out at 8 am. By 8:15, Tara, Lisa, and Beth were standing in the parking lot—somewhere between their three cars—with their yoga mats slung over their shoulders and their water bottles in hand.

"It's from that new place across from Trader Joe's," Beth answered in response to a compliment on the linen tunic she'd thrown over her yoga clothes. "In that plaza they just put up."

"That's open?" Tara asked, shaking her head at another new shopping plaza in their rapidly developing community.

"Yeah, not a lot of shops yet, but this is a cute shop next to the new sushi place."

"Oh, my sister and I got sushi there!" Lisa chimed in brightly. "It was their soft opening, so they were short staffed, but the sushi was great."

"How is your sister?" Beth asked earnestly, while Tara's face mirrored her concern.

"Still on crutches, but getting better," Lisa told them, leading in to a longer catch-up on her sister's recovery from a recent car accident.

As she wrapped up, Beth shared that her mom would need physical therapy after her upcoming knee surgery, and—after Tara and Lisa both gave her recommendations—the conversation shifted to how Tara and Lisa's kids were settling into a new school year.

By the time they moved on to weekend travel plans, it was nearly 9 am and the parking lot in front of the studio was mostly empty. Their yoga teacher, Melinda, came out of the building and flashed them a friendly smile as she headed to her car.

"Have a great day, ladies!"

As they called over goodbyes and thanks for the class, Beth looked at her watch in mock horror.

"I have a conference call at 9:30, and I still have to shower!"

Realizing the time, they scrambled toward their cars, calling last thoughts as they walked apart. As Beth drove off, Lisa called out a question about Back-to-School night, and Tara walked back to answer. Twenty minutes later, they each drove home.

On Wednesdays, they switched to Pilates, which ended at 8:30. By 8:40, they were in another parking lot, again clustered near their cars with mats slug over their shoulders and water bottles in hand.

"I don't know about that new teacher," Beth said archly, after nodding goodbye to some passing students.

"She skipped the saw," Lisa frowned, though Tara said she was okay with that omission.

"Her playlist was kind of…" Tara trailed off and the others jumped in, agreeing that it wasn't their kind of music, though maybe they'd get used to it.

"Oh!" Lisa exclaimed. "Did I tell you I'm going to a concert next weekend?" Their talk turned to upcoming events, including the axe throwing party Lisa was nervous about attending.

At 9:10, Tara was the one to jump at the time, saying, "I have a ton of emails to return before my staff meeting." And the group reluctantly parted to get on with their day.

On Fridays, they were back to yoga, but this Friday, Beth didn't show up to class. Tara and Lisa had looked for her before class and shrugged when she never appeared. As they left the building, Tara asked when Beth's mom was having knee surgery.

"Not until next week," Lisa confirmed. "Have you heard from her since Pilates?"

"She hasn't been on Facebook," Tara responded thoughtfully. "Or on Insta… I don't think."

They pulled out their phones and scrolled through a few accounts. "Not on Twitter," Lisa confirmed. "Does she use TikTok?"

"I don't think so… do you?"

"Not really," Lisa answered vaguely before shrugging and tucking her phone away. "She's probably just busy."

"Yeah," Tara agreed. "Getting ready for the beach. She is going this weekend, right?"

"That's what she said," Lisa answered with a quick nod. "A quick trip before she'd be taking care of her mom next week."

"That's right." Tara nodded uneasily, adding, "I'm sure we'll see her Monday. Or was she taking Monday off for the trip?"

"Oh," Lisa frowned. "I don't remember. But she'll definitely post pictures from the beach."

"True," Tara smiled, feeling reassured enough to change the subject, and they talked until nearly 9:30 without bringing up Beth again.

But when Monday came around, Beth was not in class again, and she hadn't posted any pictures from her weekend at the beach. She hadn't posted anything at all.

"Should we check on her?" Tara asked, as they walked out of the yoga studio and down the stairs to the parking lot.

"I messaged her this morning," Lisa sighed. "No response."

"Oh," Tara frowned. She was about to suggest that she send a message, too, but didn't want it to seem like Beth was more likely to respond to her than to Lisa.

"She read it though," Lisa continued. "At least, the app says the message was read by somebody."

"Well, then, she's probably just busy," Tara said quickly. Then, thinking about it more, she asked, "What did you say?"

"Just asked if she was coming to class," Lisa shrugged. "I didn't want to make a big deal."

"Right," Tara nodded quietly.

They'd known each other for years, chatting after classes three times a week with very few unexplained absences, though occasionally things came up and one of them didn't make it in for a while. It wasn't like they owed each other an explanation… and a gap in attendance didn't necessarily mean something was wrong…

"She'll be at Pilates," Lisa reassured, but Tara quickly shook her head.

"I think her mom has surgery that morning."

They were quiet, considering their options.

"You know where she lives, right?" Tara asked suddenly.

"Yeah, not far from me. I gave her rides that time her car was in the shop."

"So, let's check in on her," Tara suggested.

"Today?" Lisa asked in surprise. "Now?"

"It's only 8:20," Tara replied, checking her watch. "We usually talk later than this."

"I guess…" Lisa hesitated, wondering how Beth might feel about them just showing up at her house.

"We'll grab some flowers and a card," Tara rushed on, gesturing to the grocery store two doors down from the yoga studio. "As a 'hope your mom's surgery goes well' gift. And if she doesn't answer, we'll just leave them at her door."

"Huh," Lisa considered, then nodded slowly. They'd gotten coffee together a few times over the years, but that had been the extent of their socializing outside of post-workout parking lot chats. "Okay," she brightened. "Why not?"

Tara followed Lisa on the short drive to Beth's house. They all lived within 5 miles of the studio; Lisa and Beth in one direction and Tara in the other. Though Tara didn't mind driving out of her way to make their delivery together.

Beth's home was a blue townhouse with pink flowers growing in a planter beside the front door. Her car was parked in the driveway, though there was no one in sight.

After parking alongside the curb, Tara and Lisa walked up to the door together. Tara carried a potted orchid and Lisa held the card they'd both signed on the hood of her car. Lisa rang the doorbell and they waited, glancing around the quiet street, and nodding to a pair of women who passed by on the sidewalk.

A minute later, the door opened, and Beth gaped at them in disbelief. She wore a baggy t-shirt and shorts with her hair pulled up in a messy bun. Her feet were bare, and she wore glasses instead of her usual contact lenses.

"What are you—?" She stopped herself, catching sight of the orchid and card. "You brought me an orchid?"

"Uh, yeah," Tara thrust the plant toward her with straight arms.

"For you and your mom," Lisa added, holding up the card. "For good luck on the surgery."

"Oh," Beth sighed, staring at them a moment before finally reaching for the orchid. "That's so sweet of you!"

"We were worried," Tara said abruptly, feeling the emptiness in her hands as Beth received the plant.

"You weren't in class," Lisa continued, "and you haven't been posting…"

"Oh, I was busy," Beth responded, seeming a little flustered. "I mean with the beach trip, and now getting ready for mom's stay… Oh, do you want to come in? I have coffee."

Lisa and Tara exchanged a quick look. Tara's first meeting wasn't until 10 and Lisa set her own work hours. They smiled and stepped inside, kicking off their shoes and asking what they could do to help.

"Just a chat would be great," Beth grinned, stepping aside to let her friends into her home.

§

Parking Lot Friends - Ep. 32, September 7, 2021

As a yoga teacher and student, I've seen many friendships develop in the minutes before and after class. Conversations often continue into the parking lot and provide regular support for life's ups and downs.

The Goose in the House

"There's a goose in the living room!"

Sheryl's voice had the intensity of a shout but the volume of a whisper.

"What?"

Ted's question came in his normal voice as he looked up from his phone with a hint of annoyance. He was sitting at the kitchen island, trying to enjoy his morning coffee.

"Shhh!" Sheryl hushed with more force than was necessary, causing a flap of feathers followed by a scowl as Ted lowered his phone and shook his head at her.

"What is your—? Hey!" He caught sight of the goose standing a mere twelve feet away in the adjacent living room. "There's a goose in the living room!"

"Oh, really?" Sheryl liberally layered on the sarcasm. "I hadn't noticed."

The goose looked at them both in turn, then bent his long neck to casually peck at some feathers on his right wing.

"How is there a goose in the house?" Ted asked incredulously. "How long has it been here?"

"How should I know?" Sheryl hissed, somewhere between a whisper and her normal speaking voice. "You were here first! Was it here when you came downstairs?"

Ted blinked at Sheryl, glanced at the goose, glanced at his phone, glanced at his coffee, and then blinked at Sheryl again.

"I don't know."

"You don't know?"

"I don't think so… I mean, no. Of course not," Ted settled into a more confident stance. "It couldn't have been here. Not the whole time I was making coffee."

Sheryl did not seem as sure about that.

"So, it just walked in then?" She asked. "Minutes before I did?"

"Yes." Ted felt the situation called for someone to be decisive.

"Okay," Sheryl rolled her eyes and looked back at the goose.

The goose had stopped preening and was simply standing in the middle of the room.

"You don't believe me?" Ted asked, sounding injured.

"What?"

"You don't believe me that the goose walked in here minutes before you did?" He clarified needlessly as Sheryl was already pressing her lips together and shaking her head in irritation.

"That doesn't really matter now, does it?"

"It matters to me," Ted picked up his coffee and took a soothing sip.

He felt that this was too much for him first thing in the morning. It was bad enough to find a goose in the living room, but to then be disbelieved by his own wife when he'd simply asserted that he had not seen said goose until she'd arrived... Well, really.

He sighed.

Sheryl didn't care all that much how Ted felt about it, as she was preoccupied by the goose standing in the middle of their living room.

They were both silent for nearly a minute, which felt more like two.

"Is there a door open?"

Ted turned toward Sheryl, considering her question carefully.

"I didn't open one," he assured her.

"You didn't see the goose either," Sheryl muttered, going to check the front door.

"I heard that," Ted responded but not loud enough for Sheryl to hear.

The goose looked toward the kitchen doorway, as if wondering when Sheryl would be back, and Ted hoped it wasn't about to follow her around the house.

"The door is shut," Sheryl confirmed, returning to the kitchen and standing with her hands on her hips.

"I don't think you should leave again," Ted told her. "The room, I mean. I think the goose was about to follow you."

"I wish it would," Sheryl mused. "I could lead it right out the front door!"

"Should we try?" Ted set down his coffee and turned toward the living room, ready to enact the plan.

The goose settled into the carpet, fluffing its feathers as if cozying into its nest.

"Doesn't look like he's going anywhere now," Sheryl frowned.

Ted agreed glumly.

They watched the goose.

The goose watched them.

"All right," Ted drew his shoulders back. "How did that goose get in here?"

"I'm more concerned about getting it out," Sheryl insisted, crossing her arms tightly.

"Well, yes," Ted hesitated, taking a moment to consider his point. "But if we don't know how it got in here, how do we know another one won't follow it in?"

"Oh," Sheryl bit her lip worriedly. "I hadn't thought of that."

"Exactly," Ted puffed up his chest and reached for his coffee, having earned another sip.

They both thought silently, until Sheryl sidled over with an uneasy frown.

"I think we both know who it was." She spoke in her quietest whisper yet. "And there isn't anything we can do about it."

Puzzled, Ted turned his head enough to see her face without losing sight of the goose.

"We do?"

Sheryl rolled her eyes and sighed, then leaned in closer.

"It was the writer."

"The old man down the street?" Ted asked, picturing the gray-haired, shawl-collared septuagenarian who had once been a journalist and now constructed crossword puzzles for the local newspaper.

"No," Sheryl's whisper carried more of a hiss. "*The* writer."

Ted looked back toward the goose, less bothered by its resting on his living room carpet than he was by the turn in their conversation.

"You know," Sheryl prodded. "The writer who put us in this house, and gave you that coffee, and put us in these matching pajamas. She put the goose in the living room."

"Oh," Ted blinked. He looked down at the blue pajama set he was wearing and noticed that Sheryl was wearing an identical set. Long sleeved tops with white buttons. Long pants that brushed the tops of their bare feet. He thought they'd bought these pajamas last week, but maybe that was a memory the writer had put in his head.

"Why would she do that?" Ted whispered back, though he wondered why they were whispering. If the writer had put the goose in their living room, and the pajamas on their bodies, perhaps she was putting the words in their mouths as well. Were they trying to keep those words from her ears? Or from the goose?

Ted wished he had something stronger than coffee in his mug.

"I don't know," Sheryl shrugged, and Ted could see her brow furrowed in thought. "Maybe it's an experiment. Maybe she wants to see what we'll do about the goose."

"But if she's the writer…" Ted spoke slowly. "The one who creates all of this… Then how could it be an experiment? I mean, how could she watch to see how we would react…?"

They stood side by side, watching the goose.

The goose cocked its head to one side, watching to see what they would do.

Ted felt a shiver run down his spine.

Sheryl swallowed harshly.

"What if…" Ted's voice broke off. He gathered his strength and tried again. "What if there isn't a writer at all?"

His question was so preposterous that Sheryl's head swiveled to face him directly.

"No writer?"

Her whisper had become a mere mouthing of the words, but Ted was close enough to see and understand them.

"Hear me out…" He fumbled to make sense of his idea. "What if we put ourselves in this house by filling out our application and moving ourselves in? What if we bought our pajamas at the store, not because there was a story written about it, but because we just… well, went shopping and bought these pajamas?"

Sheryl regarded him skeptically.

"And the goose?" Her voice was soft, but audible. "The goose got in the house on its own? Without anyone writing it into our living room?"

"Well, I know it sounds crazy…" Ted cast around for a better explanation, then brightened with a realization. "The back bedroom! Didn't you open the window in there yesterday? You were airing it out for your sister's visit! Could you have left the window open?"

"Oh, I…"

Sheryl's eyes dropped to the floor, shifting rapidly as she thought through yesterday's actions. She did remember opening the window, and she didn't remember going back to close it, but still…

"If the window is open…" Ted's eyes lit up, considering the possibilities, but Sheryl shook her head quickly.

"That wouldn't prove anything," she insisted. "The writer could have easily written in the open window."

They both turned back to the goose.

Ted frowned, discouraged by Sheryl's unassailable logic but still tingling from his unorthodox thought.

Sheryl nodded tightly, reassuring herself that the goose was a test. A simple experiment the writer was using to enliven their day.

"We should find a way to lure it outside," Sheryl suggested calmly. "And then check that window."

"Yes," Ted agreed with a lingering sigh.

He took one more sip of coffee, set down the mug, and resolved to see where this day would take them. Just another day, like any other.

§

The Goose in the House - Ep. 4, April 6, 2021

This story went meta, without intention. I started writing without knowing why the goose was in the house and, when no other answer came, I thought, "it's there because I put it there!" I love how that led to a silly exploration of free will. In fact, I loved it enough that I revisited Sheryl and Ted in two more stories, which are are up next.

Writer's Block

Sheryl and Ted quietly sipped tea. They were sitting in their living room, side-by-side on their comfortable couch. Sunlight streamed in from a window on their right and, on the left, the room opened into their airy kitchen.

The tea was mild and just the right temperature for comfortable sipping. They wore comfortable clothes, weekend leisurewear, and appeared to be in no rush to go anywhere or do anything.

"Have you noticed how dull our lives have gotten lately?" Ted asked, peering into his ceramic mug of tea.

"Dull?" Sheryl asked, raising an eyebrow before lifting her cup for another delicate sip. "I wouldn't say our lives are dull."

"Hmm," Ted responded gently. He also took another sip of tea, though he first glanced across the room with a look of concern.

"I'm enjoying this tea," Sheryl told him, as if that settled the matter.

"Well, yes," Ted allowed. "I'm enjoying this tea also, but I wouldn't call it exciting."

Sheryl frowned.

"I didn't say the tea was exciting," she reminded him. "I said I was enjoying it."

"I know," Ted sighed. "But enjoying something doesn't mean it isn't dull."

Sheryl considered that, taking time to inhale the aroma of her tea and feel the warmth of the mug against her cupped hands.

"I don't know about that," she countered slowly. "If you're enjoying something, can it really be all that dull? Isn't dull *not enjoyable*, practically by definition?"

"I think you're missing the point," Ted said, again looking across the room with concern.

"I don't think I am," Sheryl argued.

Her tone clearly showed that she was losing patience with this conversation. "I'm simply saying that enjoying tea is not dull."

"Forget the tea," Ted snapped in exasperation.

He sat his cup on a nearby end table and turned back to Sheryl with fire in his eyes.

"When was the last time we went anywhere?" He asked pointedly. "When was the last time we traveled or went to the movies or even took a walk?"

"Well, we… uh…" Sheryl trailed off, puzzling over the answer.

"Or forget *going* anywhere," Ted went on. "When was the last time anything interesting happened right here? In our own house? Anything interesting or unusual?"

"Oh, I get it," Sheryl huffed, setting her mug down on the table beside her end of the couch. "You don't find me interesting anymore!"

"No, no!" Ted waved her hurt words away. "You are interesting. You are perfectly wonderful. But when was the last time we *did* anything interesting?"

"You think I'm perfectly wonderful?" Sheryl blushed and smiled, ignoring the rest of Ted's comment.

"Yes, of course," he told her, trying to keep his patience.

They were quiet then. Sheryl reached for her mug of tea, then set it back on the end table.

"We have been drinking a lot of tea lately," she admitted, beginning to catch a bit of Ted's concern.

"Right?" Ted encouraged. "That's all I'm saying."

He again looked across the room. This time, Sheryl's gaze followed, and she sighed heavily.

"This has happened before," she reminded softly. "And it's never lasted terribly long."

"I know, but…" Ted frowned, lightly shaking his head. "I'm getting very tired of tea."

Sheryl watched as Ted hung his head. She felt sorry for him but was afraid that saying the wrong thing would only make the situation worse.

"We kind of knew this was coming," she suggested cautiously. "When *that* showed up."

She gestured at the object across the room. It was a large block of stone roughly five feet long on each side. It took up most of the free space in the living room, crowding between two wing chairs and covering all but the top two inches of their wall-mounted TV.

The block was not barring their exit from the room. They could skirt around its rough edges to reach the kitchen and the rest of the house, including the front door. The block was not keeping them where they were… except that it kind of was keeping them there.

Despite its nondescript features, the huge gray block was mesmerizing. Whatever else they tried to do, Sheryl and Ted soon found themselves back on the couch, sipping tea and looking at the stone block. Looking at it, but not talking about it. Until today.

"It's pretty obvious," Ted noted sadly.

"Oh, extremely obvious," Sheryl agreed. "But that's the point, isn't it? Or part of the point?"

"What is?" Ted studied Sheryl curiously before catching her meaning. "Oh, you mean, the point of a writer putting a large block in the center of our living room to indicate writer's block *is* such an obvious point because the writer's own writer's block is limiting her creativity?"

"Ted!" Sheryl hissed warningly, glancing toward the ceiling as if afraid they'd be overhead.

"Oh, please," Ted scoffed. "Do you think the writer doesn't *know* she has writer's block?"

"Well, she does now," Sheryl muttered, beginning to chew her lower lip.

"I don't see why we're supposed to tiptoe around the writer when *her* issues are affecting *our* lives."

"Ted, please," Sheryl begged. Ted was now standing, getting bolder by the minute, even as Sheryl looked around the room with growing fear.

"You know I'm right," Ted insisted. "I get that there's a writer creating the whole world and spinning out the stories of our lives… I mean, it would be pretty crazy to think otherwise… Like, what? Like those people who think we just do whatever we want without any kind of guiding direction?

"Anyway, wait… What was I saying?"

"That you know there's a writer creating our world and spinning out the stories of our lives…" Sheryl repeated, drawing his monologue back on track.

"Right, thanks. I know that, but maybe the events she creates in our lives are partly up to us to interpret."

Sheryl stopped biting her lip and blinked at Ted's suggestion. She stood up and studied the stone, trying to see it in a new light.

"But whenever this block has appeared before, our lives have gotten…"

"Dull," Ted finished.

"Less busy," Sheryl corrected weakly. "There's never anything…."

"Interesting," Ted supplied.

"Out of the ordinary," Sheryl amended. "So, it does stand to reason that if the writer *writes* less whenever there's a large block in our house…"

"Yes, it makes sense." Ted jumped in, saving her from finishing the uncomfortable thought. "But maybe we only *think* that because we lack the creativity needed to see the potential in the block."

"What?"

Ted rubbed his hands together as he excitedly cast his eyes around the room.

"Well… maybe…" He drew the thought out until his eyes caught on the fireplace at the far side of the living room. "The writer puts the block here to see what we'll do with it."

"Like a test?" Sheryl questioned, beginning to understand Ted's reasoning. "To see if we'll interact with the block in some interesting way?"

Ted pulled an iron poker from the set of fireside tools and tested its weight in his hands.

"Oh, but Ted!" Sheryl's cheeks flamed as she realized what he was about to do.

"It's time we took matters into our own hands!" Ted exclaimed, stepping forward and raising the poker over his head.

"But, Ted…?" Sheryl's quiet voice caught Ted just before he took a swing at the stone.

He turned to her, a look of impatience chasing the glee from his face.

"If the writer writes everything we do… isn't she writing what you're doing now?"

Ted lowered the poker, knowing Sheryl was right.

They stood quietly. Ted stared at the floor between his feet. It wasn't the first time he'd gotten caught up in a thought like that. Blurring the lines between what the writer might or might not control, but ultimately accepting that she was behind everything.

"Oh!" Sheryl perked up with a clap of her hands. "Ted, think about it! If the stone block does indicate writer's block… you wanting to smash the block must mean the writer is ready to move past it!"

"Huh," Ted slowly began to grin. He tapped the heavy poker against his open palm and eyed the block with renewed excitement. "That makes sense."

"Well…?" Sheryl urged. "What are you waiting for?"

With a triumphant laugh, Ted lifted the poker overhead and smashed it onto the block. A large chunk of stone cracked off an upper corner, revealing the curved edge of an object that seemed to be embedded within.

"Keep going!" Sheryl cried, then stepped forward, extending her palm. "No, wait, give me a turn!"

For the next several minutes, they passed the poker, taking turns as they chipped away at the massive block. The air filled with fine dust and the floor became littered with chunks of stone. When they were finished, they stepped back to survey their work.

A stone creature sat where the block had been. It had the look of a woodland nymph or elf, but with androgynous features and a drawstring bag slung over one shoulder. A stone butterfly rested on the creature's upturned palm and a bird perched on its opposite arm. All in all, it was a lovely statue.

"We'll put it in the garden!" Sheryl exclaimed with another happy clap.

"Near the rose bushes," Ted agreed, smiling proudly at their new creation.

"And we'll have a party to show it off to our friends!"

"Yes, a barbecue!" Ted beamed, his mouth already watering at the thought of charred beef.

"And you were afraid our lives were getting dull…" Sheryl teased lightly.

"Yeah, yeah," Ted shrugged, feeling his cheeks turn pink.

"You just need a little faith," Sheryl told him.

"And patience," Ted agreed, returning her warm smile.

They brushed the stone dust from their hands, ready to get on with their party plans.

§

Writer's Block - Ep. 19, June 29, 2021

This prompt was chosen because I wanted to revisit Sheryl, Ted, and the writer from episode 4, *The Goose in the House.* Yet, it was still free-written with no planning beyond a prompt that included the word *writer.* It was fun to explore the idea of writer's block, a concept I rarely consider. When I'm struggling to find words, I just start writing, accepting that it won't be my best work, but I can fix it later.

Duck à l'Orange

"Oh, not again!"

Sheryl walked into the front hall, saw Ted kneeling by what appeared to be a goose wearing an orange coat, and turned to go back into the kitchen.

"Wait!" Ted called after her with a laugh. "It's a duck not a goose!"

"Like that's better?" Sheryl shuddered, averting her eyes as she remembered the morning she'd come downstairs to find a goose in their living room.

"It's not a real duck," Ted assured, still laughing lightly. "It's a statue for the garden."

"Oh."

Sheryl peered around him at the white duck in an orange coat.

"His name is Al," Ted said proudly. "Al Orange."

"Oh," Sheryl repeated with even less enthusiasm.

"Get it?" Ted persisted. "He's a duck, wearing an orange coat, and his name is Al Orange. You know, like duck à l'orange?"

"Yeah," Sheryl sighed. "I get it."

"Oh, come on!" Ted laughed. "That's hilarious."

"I need more coffee." Sheryl headed back into the kitchen.

Ted followed with Al Orange tucked awkwardly beneath one arm. Sheryl frowned at the statue, keeping her distance as she poured coffee into a yellow mug. She had a pretty good idea what was going on, and she wasn't about to get involved.

Ted set the stone duck on the kitchen island and brushed a bit of lint from his orange coat.

"Should I put him by the azaleas or back by that patch of daisies?"

"I don't care," Sheryl told him, after a long swig of coffee. "Just please get him off the island before he comes to life and tears up the place."

"What?" Ted chuckled, still admiring the duck. "He's pretty realistic, but I don't think we have to worry about that!"

"Don't we?" Sheryl wasn't convinced. She skirted the island, heading toward the back door. "Let's just put him outside and be done with it."

"You're in a mood," Ted frowned, annoyed at Sheryl's response.

"I'm not," Sheryl retorted, crossing her arms petulantly.

"You are," Ted insisted "I come in with a perfectly good duck for the garden and you're in a mood about him."

"I'm not in a mood about him," Sheryl responded through clenched teeth.

"Oh, yeah, this isn't a mood?" He crossed his arms and clenched his jaw in a fair imitation of Sheryl's defensive position. Sheryl dropped her arms and flapped her hands nervously.

"Oh, everything is a mood to you!" She snapped crossly.

"Huh, well, I suppose that's true," Ted nodded thoughtfully. "I mean, anything anyone is feeling at any time is their mood of the moment."

"Exactly," Sheryl agreed triumphantly, as if she'd made a crucial point. "I'm in a mood. You're in a mood. Everyone's in a mood all the time. But my mood isn't the mood you think it is."

Ted cocked his head, looking from her to the stone duck. At some point, he'd lost the thread of the conversation and could only nod in vague agreement.

"So, you're in a good mood?" He ventured uneasily.

"Yes. Yes, of course, I am," Sheryl agreed, glancing toward the sky as if afraid she'd wouldn't be believed by an invisible listener.

"Okay," Ted frowned, then shook away whatever thought had half-formed in his mind. "So, you like Al Orange?"

"Yes, he's a lovely duck," Sheryl agreed and quickly opened the back door. "Now go get him settled and we can have some tea."

Ted started to pick up the duck, then left him on the island as he looked up at Sheryl with a gleam of realization.

"Oh, I get it," he told her. "You think this duck is a gift from *her*."

"What? No," Sheryl scoffed, glancing back at the sky nervously.

"She didn't send us the duck," Ted reassured. "I went out and bought the duck myself."

"Okay, good," Sheryl told him, gesturing toward the open door. "So, let's get him into the garden."

"You don't believe me." Ted sounded hurt. "You think he's a gift from her. But she only sends us weird things. Like that live goose or that big stone block. Al Orange isn't… Wait a minute! You don't like Al Orange! You think he's weird!"

Sheryl paled and her eyes grew wide.

"I never said that." She bit her lip and glanced at the duck in the orange coat with a forced smile.

"You don't like Al Orange!" Ted accused again. "You think the only way he'd show up is if *she* sent him here. You don't think I'd buy him myself. Even when I told you I did."

"Yeah, but, Ted…" Sheryl tried for a soothing tone. "We've been over this before. She's the *writer*."

"I know." Ted looked down and sheepishly kicked his foot against the linoleum.

Sheryl lowered her voice. "And the writer is the one who makes all of… this… happen."

She gestured around the room, indicating their house, their town, and their whole lives.

"Well, yeah," Ted agreed, still looking down.

"So, the writer did bring the duck here, even if you bought the duck. The writer *wrote* that you bought the duck."

Ted sighed and resolutely raised his gaze.

"Yeah, well, the writer *wrote* for you to drink coffee, too."

Sheryl's lips pressed into a firm line. She didn't have a good response but felt that he was wrong and was crossing a line with that suggestion.

"She did," Ted insisted, seeing Sheryl's eye twitch in response. "If she wrote me going to the store, she wrote you drinking coffee. And she wrote you getting dressed and having breakfast… And she wrote you opening the door and standing there next to it. So, what does it matter if she wrote me buying the duck?"

"Well, it…" Sheryl floundered. "You're taking it a bit far. We don't *know* that she writes all of that, exactly. I mean, she does, of course. But the simple stuff, the everyday stuff doesn't matter so much. It's when she gets bored and writes in something weird that—"

"Aha!" Ted interrupted, thrusting a finger in the air. "You do think Al Orange is weird!"

"It's a stone duck wearing an orange coat!" Sheryl cried in exasperation. "And you've named him Al Orange!"

"So? I like Al Orange. I think it's the perfect name for a duck."

They stared at each other across the kitchen. Sheryl glanced back at Al Orange, making sure he was still a stone duck. Nothing more.

"She does this to get a rise out of us," Sheryl muttered softly.

Ted shook his head, though he knew she was right. They'd known for some time that the writer seemed to let them be for long stretches only to pop in with a strange object when she was bored. They suspected she did it to see how they would react. Although, if she was the one writing everything they did and said…?

Ted's head began to hurt the way it always did when he gave the writer too much thought.

"Maybe we shouldn't give her the satisfaction," Ted answered in an equally quiet voice.

Their eyes met across the kitchen, this time in silent agreement.

"Shall we put Al Orange near the daisies?" Sheryl asked brightly.

"That's a good idea," Ted agreed with relief. "And then we can have some tea."

"I would love some tea," Sheryl agreed, smiling as she followed Ted and the duck out the back door.

§

Duck à l'Orange - Ep. 49, January 18, 2022

This is the third and (so far) last story involving Sheryl, Ted, and the writer. That wasn't my intention when I chose the prompt, but it's what came out when I said the prompt out loud (in a bad French accent) and thought it sounded like a duck named Al Orange. It seemed like a joke Ted would make and since a goose first brought them into existence, I liked the idea of giving them a duck.

Unicorns and Rainbows

The lavender grass in the pasture took on a more vibrant hue as the sun rose in the pink and blue sky. The gently rolling hills of the countryside stretched for miles, broken only by the small stone house and the larger enclosure where the unicorns could shelter as needed. Of course, the unicorns rarely used their covered home as they preferred to sleep under a starry sky.

Arwyn also enjoyed sleeping under the stars on occasion, though most nights, she was happy to nestle into her feather tick beneath a quilt of woven silk. She woke early each morning, before the peacocks' daybreak warbling, and began her day with a leisurely walk through the unicorn pasture.

The unicorns adored Arwyn nearly as much as she loved them. Each morning, human and animal alike looked forward to their graceful ritual of greeting. As Arwyn strolled over the lavender grass, the unicorns unfolded their silvery limbs and rose to accept her gentle pats and friendly caresses. Their work would come later in the day, when the sun reached its full height and Arwyn was prepared to gather the clouds. For now, they simply enjoyed each other's quiet presence.

Arwyn came from a long line of rainbow farmers and she was well suited to the job. While some of her ancestors had used gruff demands and appeals of authority to collect their harvest, Arwyn believed it was better to coax the unicorns with gracious requests and genuine affection. Her approach was inarguably the better method, as the farm had never had a more abundant yield and the gods were pleased with the brighter colors and longer endurance of her patiently gathered rainbows.

Yet, rainbow farming was difficult work. Gathering the clouds required a tremendous effort, and that was before the arduous task of wringing out just enough rain to release the brightest, happiest rainbows from her precious herd of unicorns.

The unicorns knew how hard the work was on Arwyn—though she never complained—and their love for her made them want her to succeed. As soon as the gentle rain fell, they gladly offered up their purest light, allowing vibrant rainbows to arc across the pure blue sky.

Above the clouds, the gods eagerly accepted these colored ribbons of light. They stored the rainbows away in crystal vials so they could be released in other locations at just the right auspicious occasions. It was a piece of god-craft that most humans knew nothing about. They were all too happy to interpret the rainbows as gifts from the gods, without ever knowing where the gods had harvested them.

Arwyn did not mind having a hidden role in this cosmic process. She, like the rainbow farmers before her, was content to live out her days among the unicorns. She knew she would one day meet a partner who would settle with her to raise a family and pass her knowledge to their own children.

For now, Arwyn lived in the quiet between generations. Her own parents had recently passed, and she had no siblings. This was not unusual among rainbow farmers. They often had only one child, or two children at most. Too many could lead to conflicts in running a farm and there were few places where a grown child could strike out to begin a new rainbow farm of their own.

Most rainbow farmers kept to themselves, outside of market days, and their unicorns rarely strayed beyond the undefined barriers of their own pastures. However, there was nothing to keep them on the farm, and unicorns did occasionally travel to other farmlands.

One morning, Arwyn was surprised to find a new unicorn resting just beyond the edge of her herd. She approached the creature cautiously, holding out her hand and offering warm murmurs of welcome. She had no way of knowing where the unicorn had been before or how long it would stay in her pasture, though she was pleased by its presence.

That afternoon, Arwyn strode to the center of the pasture with more purpose. She had completed her morning meditations and was ready to gather the clouds.

This difficult task took great concentration, and so Arwyn had put any thoughts of the new unicorn aside. She lifted her strong arms wide and turned in a slow circle. The circle expanded as she wove her way between the unicorns, using intricate flicks of her wrists and hands to coax the clouds together. As the circle grew, her pace increased. Her steps became a delicate dance as her skirt swished and her upper body swayed.

The unicorns smiled to see her weave her way between them. They could feel her love and gratitude as she passed. They could see the effort she expended to draw just the right number of clouds overhead.

The sun peeked gently between the clouds, lighting them from above even as their swell of rain darkened them from below. Back in the center of the pasture, Arwyn's sweeping gestures held the clouds in place. Her fingers pulsed in a delicate clench and release, encouraging the clouds to release crystal drops of rain across the purple pasture.

As the warm drops began to fall, the unicorns glowed in pleasure. Arwyn let her gaze flit across her beloved friends as waves of light lifted from their silvery backs. Red, orange, yellow, green, blue, indigo, and violet. Each unicorn released waves of colored light, letting them rise through the clouds where they joined in graceful arcs. Each unicorn, that is, except one.

When Arwyn looked toward the edge of the pasture, she saw the new unicorn standing alone, shy and uncertain. Their eyes met, and Arwyn understood. This new unicorn had come from a farm where the rainbow ritual was quite different. Likely a farm where the unicorns had been lined up, assigned colors, and ordered to produce those colors on command.

It was a common practice in most farms, and while the new unicorn had not particularly enjoyed the process, he was startled to find himself in a place where there seemed to be no such order. He stood aside, wondering which color he was meant to produce and when he was meant to produce it. The freedom around him felt like chaos and he was unhappy.

Arwyn saw all this in a single glance and her heart was troubled. For a moment, the rain faltered and the air dimmed. The steady stream of rising colors paused as the unicorns glanced from Arwyn to the new unicorn.

The new unicorn bristled under the attention, a prickling feeling of unease spreading through his shaky limbs, but it was short-lived. Arwyn shook off her moment of concern and offered the new unicorn a radiant smile of welcome. With an encouraging glance among the others, she redoubled her efforts to draw the soft rain from the gathered clouds.

The unicorns nearest their new visitor stepped closer to him, gently releasing their colors into the damp sky. He saw that they gave their colors without direction. They gave their colors freely. Looking back at Arwyn, he saw that she was content to have him with them whether he produced his own colors or not.

A warmth spread through the new unicorn, replacing the quake of unease he'd felt just moments before. He watched the joy in the unicorns around him, felt the softness of the clouds' rain, and released a symphony of color, smiling as his own offering joined to form a brilliant rainbow against the pure blue sky.

§

Unicorns and Rainbows - Ep. 21, July 6, 2021

Unicorns and rainbows go together like peanut butter and jelly or hot chocolate and marshmallows. Once I put unicorns in a pasture, it seemed obvious that it would be set on a rainbow farm. Well, obvious in my mind. While I didn't plan to revisit Arwyn and her unicorns, I stumbled into it when writing the next story, *Fireside Wine Chat*.

Fireside Wine Chat

Igmara propped her sturdy axe by the cabin door and brushed a fallen leaf from her thick, braided hair. The days had become crisp, and the leaves had taken on their autumn hues of russet, gold, and fiery red. The naiads retreated earlier each day, giving the dark night over to the roving banshees.

As Igmara unlaced her boots, her eyes drifted toward the stone fireplace, and she smiled softly to herself. The shorter days had charms beyond their autumn leaves. At least for those skilled in the art of pyromancy.

Though before she could settle by the fireside, Igmara had a few evening chores to complete. She hung her cloak on a peg by the door and slipped into her soft-soled house shoes. She fetched a metal pail from beneath her sink and began filling it with rose-colored seed from a bag in the pantry.

Like most homes in N'yeardwahl, the main room of Igmara's cabin had a kitchen clustered in one corner and large wooden table suitable for meals, crafts, and social gatherings. There were two stuffed chairs opposite the large stone fireplace and a small table between them.

The far wall, opposite the kitchen, included an enclosed bathroom beneath her bedroom loft. Beside the bathroom, a metal door etched with runic symbols led beyond the main room.

Igmara carried her filled bucket of seed toward the metal door, pausing to straighten a painting that had become crooked on the rough-hewn cabin wall. The painted was a cherished gift from Fleura, a faun who had recently moved to N'yeardwahl and was fast becoming one of Igmara's closest local friends. Not that she had many close friends in N'yeardwahl.

Igmara unlocked and opened the metal door, using care to avoid spilling seed from her full bucket. The room behind the metal door was brightly lit, despite the darkening sky. Metal braziers hung from chains along the peak of the long room's thick glass roof, yet the dancing flames did not add much heat to the stone-walled stable below. This was by design, as the stable had to be kept at a precise temperature for the health and comfort of the miniature griffons.

While there were times when Igmara housed a dozen or more griffins, for the time being, there were only six creatures lolling around the straw-covered stone floor or standing on powerful back legs to peer out the room's high windows. Igmara scanned the stable for the seventh griffon and quickly found him perched on a ledge just below the tall glass ceiling.

Like most griffons, Igmara's miniature breed featured the body, back legs, and tail of a lion along with the head, wings, and front talons of an eagle. The most visible difference was in their size, which was significantly smaller than a typical griffin, making them about the same size as a medium goat. The less visible difference was in their diet. Unlike most breeds, Igmara's miniature griffons were herbivores. Specifically, they were raised on the high-protein rose-colored seed Igmara grew in a pasture on her farm.

As Igmara made her way about the stable, ladling seed into wooden bowls, the griffins eagerly approached for their dinner. Even Bastian, the quiet griffin who had retreated to his lofty perch, soon swooped to the ground in a lazy arc.

Igmara spoke to the griffins lovingly as she doled out their seed and sat back to watch them enjoy dinner. "Did you have a nice afternoon?" she began simply, not expecting an answer. "Did you see the silly naiads playing catch with the pinecones?"

She turned toward the nearest window, seeing that the sky was nearly full dark. It would soon be time to light the fire.

After spending some time lightly smoothing feathers and scratching furry backs, Igmara gathered her empty bucket and bid the griffins good evening. She had tried not to rush her time with them, but it had been hard to stay calm as the first stars blazed in the sky above.

With her chores finished, Igmara added another log to the grate in the fireplace and set the kindling ablaze. As she waited for the larger logs to catch, Igmara fetched a bottle of wine from the kitchen, poured out a single glass, and set both bottle and glass on the small table between the two fireside chairs.

Her last task was to unbind a leather pouch from her belt and sprinkle a mound of iridescent powder into her cupped hand. She held the powder near to her heart and closed her eyes, waiting to sense the moment of connection. It came quickly, and Igmara tossed the sparkling powder into the flickering flames. As she turned, one of the fireside chairs was no longer empty.

Igmara's smile stretched wide as she took her place beside the shimmering form of her dearest friend, Arwyn. She lifted her glass in toast and they drank with contented sighs.

"How are the griffins?" Arwyn asked, knowing that Igmara had recently released a new generation into the wild.

"They're well enough," Igmara answered mildly. "Though Bastion seems a bit down."

"Hmm," Arwyn murmured sympathetically. Her own unicorns had more freedom to come and go as they'd please, though she understood why breeding griffins were safer being stabled until their numbers grew in the wild.

"But tell me what else is new!" Igmara insisted brightly. "Have you been to the market since fall began?"

"Yes, yes," Arwyn laughed, sharing her friend's love of autumnal baked goods and housewares. "And Marlyanna had created a warm pumpkin spiced cider that is divine."

"Oh, I had a similar brew at our market!" Igmara nearly sloshed her wine out of her glass in excitement, causing them both to laugh again. "It was delicately spiced with cinnamon and nutmeg, and I know not what else. Divine is the word for it."

"Speaking of divine…" Arwyn began with contained excitement. "The gods have been so pleased with my unicorns' rainbow production that they've rewarded me with a fine young phoenix."

"A phoenix?" Igmara squealed. "Oh, that's wonderful!"

"Yes, and she's quite beautiful," Arwyn confided. "Come see for yourself."

Igmara turned toward the fireplace and let her gaze soften into the flames. After a slow blink, Igmara's glowing form sat beside Arwyin, in her second fireside chair. Igmara let her eyes drift around the interior of Arwyn's cozy stone house until she caught sight of the brilliant red and gold plumage of the phoenix resting on a wooden perch.

"She's gorgeous!" Igmara told her friend, feeling pride in Arwyn's well-deserved recognition.

"Her name is Cyra." Arwyn took a slow sip of her wine as Igmara admired her new pet. After a moment, she cocked her head to one side and listened intently. "Are those banshees I hear?"

"Oh, yes," Igmara answered with a heavy sigh. "They do like to screech on autumn evenings. Though they should be winding down soon."

"I do not miss banshees," Arwyn said with a delicate shudder. It was the closest she would come to criticizing any living creature, and Igmara remembered when Arwyn had been teased by banshees during an all too rare visit.

"It's been too long since we've met in person," Igmara intoned sadly, then smiled gently, as if trying not to allow sadness into their fireside wine chat.

"I know," Arwyn replied with the same wistful expression. "Perhaps in the spring?"

"Perhaps," Igmara agreed without much conviction.

There was a moment of quiet before both friends shook it away, letting their eyes meet with a glint of connection.

"Until then, we have the fire."

Arwyn held up her wine glass in invitation. Igmara's glowing form brought her glass close, seeing its diaphanous edge pass slightly through Arwyn's solid glass just as she knew that Arwyn—back in her cabin—saw her shimmering glass cross the border of Igmara's wine glass.

Pyromancy allowed the illusion of being in the same room, the sights the sounds, but not the touch of a physical visit.

"To the fire!" Igmara smiled brightly.

"To the long nights of autumn!" Arwyn returned cheerfully.

And they settled in for an evening of chatting and drinking wine by their cozy firesides.

§

Fireside Wine Chat - Ep. 33, September 14, 2021

When I started writing this story, I thought Igmara would have a friend join her by the fireside. But making it a fantasy setting reminded me of Arwyn the rainbow farmer, which led to the idea of a long-distance friendship and a mystical fireside that allowed for a virtual visit.

Rain or Shine

"Hello?"

"Hello! *Le Petit Chou Bistro*. How may I help you?"

"Oh, hello. Yes, uh," Patty checked her notes, though she already knew what she wanted to say. "I'd like to make a reservation for six, please. On your patio. Your *covered* patio."

"Ah, *oui*. I can help you with that. When would you like to dine with us?"

Patty again checked her notes.

"On the 16th, please. Of October. This Saturday."

"Very good, madame. What time of day?"

"Oh, right!" Patty swallowed nervously. "Do you have anything at 2 o'clock? For a late lunch."

There was a pause as the woman presumably checked for availability. Patty fidgeted with the scrap of paper in her hand. She did not like making phone calls.

"Yes, we have a table for six available on the patio this Saturday at 2 o'clock."

"Oh, good!"

Patty breathed a sigh of relief.

"I was hoping you would. It's kind of last minute, but it's my sister's birthday, and she didn't want to do anything to celebrate, but then she wished we'd planned something, and I know she loves your food, so I decided to surprise her with a small lunch, just for a few friends."

"Lovely," the woman noted politely.

"But nothing special!" Patty rushed on. "I mean, she wouldn't want a fuss, so it's not an actual *party* or anything. Though some people might bring gifts, but she wouldn't want you to sing or anything."

"Of course," the woman responded kindly. "We do not sing to our guests at *Le Petit Chou Bistro,* so that will not be a problem."

"Oh, yeah, of course."

Patty laughed awkwardly, feeling the heat in her cheeks. She had never been to *Le Petit Chou Bistro* and wasn't sure what to expect.

"We could arrange a small cake if you would like?" the woman offered, pulling Patty out of her embarassed silence.

"Oh, I suppose that could be nice." Patty reflected on the offer for a moment before making her decision. "Yes, let's do that. A simple cake. We won't put her age on it or anything."

"But, of course," the woman agreed.

After her answer, Patty realized that they couldn't put her sister's age on the cake, since she hadn't told them how old she would be. She almost mentioned that but realized it wasn't all that necessary.

"The cake will simply say *Happy Birthday,*" the woman supplied, when the silence had again stretched between them.

"Yes, okay."

Patty looked back at her notes and saw where she'd scrawled the word *rain* with a question mark.

"Oh, I did say your *covered* patio, didn't I?"

There was a slight pause before the woman confirmed, "*Oui*, madame, we only have the one patio and it is covered."

"So, it will be covered if it rains?" Patty asked awkwardly, wanting to be sure.

"It will be covered rain or shine," the woman agreed pleasantly.

"That was a silly question, wasn't it?" Patty laughed again but didn't wait for an answer. "I don't make reservations like this very often. I mean, planning a party like this. Not that it's a party... but, you know, for a... special occasion."

"You are doing very well," the woman encouraged, with a touch of amusement.

"You might know my sister," Patty blurted out. "She eats there a lot. Carol Blindell? Tall, thin, blonde? Likes to toss her hair around when she talks?"

"I'm sorry, no," the woman replied patiently. "She does not sound familiar to me."

"Oh, okay."

Patty felt a curious sense of relief.

"Perhaps I'll recognize her in person," the woman added generously.

"Perhaps," Patty agreed vaguely, half wishing she'd chosen a restaurant where there wasn't a chance of her sister being recognized.

"Is there anything else I can help you with?"

Patty knew that the woman was winding down their conversation, but her tone did not sound particularly rushed. In fact, she sounded as if she would genuinely not mind if they continued to talk a few more minutes if that would put Patty's mind at ease.

Or… that's how Patty interpreted her tone.

"Do you know which table we'll be seated at?" Patty asked, trying to visualize the picture she'd seen on their website before calling.

"Ah, no…" the woman hesitated. "Is there a particular table you would like?"

"Well, I haven't been there," Patty clarified, "so I wouldn't know exactly… but I think Carol would like a table at the edge of the patio. Overlooking the lake."

"I can arrange for that," the woman responded agreeably. "We have a lovely table for six at the back corner of the patio. It offers a view of the lake, as well as the garden to the south of the restaurant."

"And it's still covered?" Patty asked urgently. "It's not so close to the edge that rain will blow in on the table?"

"One moment…"

As another pause stretched, Patty felt her palms grow damp and her stomach clench. She could just picture Carol saying, *This would be a lovely table if it weren't for the rain!*

The woman came back on the line, speaking smoothly into the quiet.

"There is currently no rain in the forecast for this Saturday. However, if it should rain, the table is sufficiently covered from the damp."

"You must think I'm very silly," Patty returned, deciding to lean into her awkwardness in hopes of diffusing it.

"Not at all," the woman assured cheerily. "It's lovely that you want to arrange a nice lunch for your sister."

"Yes, well…"

Patty bit her lip and let the scrap of paper flutter out of her hand.

Her eyes went out of focus as she remembered past family celebrations with her sister. She scarcely heard the woman ask her another question before a string of thoughts came tumbling out of her mouth.

"We don't get along all that well," she confessed.

"Or, I mean, we do, but not really. You know how it can be? She's always been *better* than me… in the things that matter to her. You know? She was always the center of attention. The baby of the family. The one who couldn't do anything wrong. You know?"

Patty rushed on, emboldened by the woman's patient listening.

"And one time we did have a party where it rained. It was her 10th birthday, and it was at this beautiful park. She'd planned to have all sorts of games—tag and three-legged races and all that—but then it rained, and we had to stay under the pavilion the whole party.

"So, Dad ran to a nearby store for coloring books and crayons, while Mom set up a game of Bingo, and I taught her friends a dance I'd learned at camp. Everyone was having fun, except Carol. She pouted, and whined, and kept standing at the edge of the pavilion and complaining that the rain was hitting her. It was so miserable, she ended up getting a second party the next weekend just to make it up to her."

Patty shook away the memory and looked down at her phone. It was still on speaker with the time of the call steadily counting away, but the woman made no response.

"Um, hello?" Patty twisted her hands together, mortified at what she's said.

After a moment of silence that felt like an hour, the woman's voice came back on the line.

"Madame? Thank you for holding. We have a reservation for six on the patio, this Saturday at 2 o'clock, and a cake that says *Happy Birthday*. Can I help with anything else?"

"No, thank you," Patty murmured softly.

"Very well," the woman returned pleasantly. "We will see you Saturday, rain or shine!"

"Yeah, see you then," Patty echoed. "Rain or shine."

§

Rain or Shine - Ep. 38, October 12, 2021

The dark sky of an impending storm inspired the prompt for this story. It was also written soon after I had made reservations for a birthday party, though my reservation had been made over text and was nowhere near this awkward. Well... maybe a little.

Pumpkin Spice

The leaf was brittle, barely holding together in the gentle fall breeze. Dina held it by the stem, watching as small pieces cracked apart and fluttered toward the leaf-strewn ground. She was deep in the forest, alone with thoughts which were also cracked and brittle. As the breeze blew and the sun warmed her face, Dina felt pieces of her thoughts fluttering away. Soon her mind would be completely clear.

She loosened her fingers, letting the dry leaf drop to the ground. And it all came back.

They were buying lattes. Not pumpkin spice because they weren't that basic. Or maybe they were, Dina thought, because they were shunning a drink they'd once loved. Was that the new basic? Following the trend of not being basic?

Dina wasn't very good at keeping up with that sort of thing. Carol was better at it which was why Dina let her order their drinks. Chai something with a pump of cold brew or… whatever it was. Dina would have been happy with black coffee.

The drinks were only their first stop that day. Lattes to gather fuel for a day of shopping. Dina had a new apartment—her first without a roommate—and Carol was going to help her decorate it in style.

Like the coffee shop, the home store was also decked out in pumpkin spice. Seasonal gourds and buffalo plaid, dried flowers and faux fall leaves. Wooden signs with rustic fonts urged them to gather together, be grateful, be cozy. Glass candle holders shouted *sweater weather*, *happy harvest*, and, yes, *pumpkin spice.*

Weaving through the russet and gold labyrinth, Carol led them to a non-seasonal section where jewel tones reigned. There were deep purples, fuchsias, emeralds, and cobalt blues. She picked up a beaded magenta throw pillow and thrust it toward Dina like an award.

"This!" she proclaimed. "This is our inspiration to build your color palette. We'll stick with similar shades, and it will be beautiful."

"I don't like pink," Dina told her, taking a step back from the vibrant pillow.

"It's not pink," Carol corrected. "It's magenta. Though pink would be perfect with it."

"I don't know." Dina shook her head, wrinkling her nose at the sea of bright colors. "I was thinking more neutral shades, earth tones. Maybe a little deep red or warm orange?"

"Seriously?" Dina scoffed. "You want the whole pumpkin spice theme? Should we grab some fake pumpkins and a cornucopia while we're here?"

"I don't mean a fall-theme, just earthy colors." Dina glanced around shyly, noticing that their only earth-tone displays did all seem to be bathed in fall décor.

"It's your apartment," Carol sighed, throwing her hands in the air. "Show me what you like. And please don't take us to modern farmhouse."

Dina frowned.

She did like a touch of modern farmhouse style but didn't want to admit it.

They wandered through the aisles, and Carol stayed quiet, arms crossed over her chest. As they walked deeper into the store, they stopped seeing salespeople or other shoppers. The aisles became more crowded, packed with sale items from previous seasons.

Just beyond an aisle of marked-down beach towels and plastic palm trees, Dina came upon two shelves stacked with throw pillows and blankets in sandy beiges and creamy off-whites. Some with touches of maroon or wine red. They were exactly what she wanted, without all the autumn trimmings.

Carol lifted a small pillow assessingly, and Dina knew she didn't approve. But before either could comment, Dina caught sight of something in the space where the pillow had been.

"What is that?" she asked, shifting pillows and blankets aside.

"Is it a door?" Carol asked, though it was clear to see that it was a door.

It was a very strange door. Narrow and wooden with an iron handle. And covered by the two wheeled shelves.

Making sure no one else was around, she and Carol cautiously eased the shelves apart.

"Is it locked?" Carol asked.

"I don't know," Dina answered.

"You should check," Carol urged.

"You should check," Dina countered.

"It's your door!" Carol insisted, stepping back a bit.

"How is it my door?" Dina asked, though she did feel a connection to the door.

"It's behind these bizarre shelves that magically have exactly what you were looking for," Carol pointed out, sounded a little affronted by the discovery.

"It's not magic," Dina said, without much conviction. "It's just a door. Probably to an old storeroom or something."

"Uh-huh," Carol shrugged, unconvinced. "So, open it and see."

There was a challenge in Carol's words and Dina felt a surge of energy. Maybe it was her door—her *magical* door—and maybe she should open it.

With a burst of courage, Dina reached out and pulled on the iron handle. The wooden door was heavy. She pulled harder, leaning back for leverage, and Carol laughed.

"Oh, forget it," she dismissed the strange door with a wave of her manicured hand. "This is too weird. Let's go back to the good part of the store. We can forget the magenta and go with purples. Violets and lilacs and a deep aubergine."

But Dina wasn't ready to give up. She liked the décor she'd found at the back of the store, and she didn't think the mysterious door was weird. It was her door. She knew it for sure the moment she'd touched the handle and she wasn't about to let go.

With a great heave, Dina yanked the door into motion. It swung open with a low creak, revealing a glow of gentle sunlight.

"What in the world…?" Carol leaned closer, peering into the golden forest beyond the door. "How is that possible…?"

Dina had no answers, but she stepped confidently through the door and spread her arms wide, basking in the sunlight that filtered through the fall foliage. She heard the crunch of dried leaves as Carol followed her into the mystical forest.

"This is crazy…" she said breathlessly. But there was no denying that they were standing in a beautiful autumn forest hidden inside a home store.

"So, I was right!" Carol laughed.

Dina looked at her in confusion.

"It's your door, your forest, hidden in shelves of your favorite style," Carol explained with a smirk.

"Look at this place! You really do love all that pumpkin spice stuff!"

Dina's face flushed and her eyes flashed.

"What's wrong with pumpkin spice?" she snapped, snatching a handful of dried leaves from the ground. "What wrong with any of the things I like?"

"What?" Carol's smile faded.

"Maybe I do like pumpkin spice lattes, and fall colors, and knee-high boots, and sweaters… And maybe the things I like are just as good as the things you like!"

Dina had never spoken to Carol like that before.

"Well… I…" Carol stuttered, then pulled herself together. "You can like whatever you want. I was just trying to improve your style."

With a frustrated shout, Dina threw her handfuls of leaves at Carol. They fluttered over her, clinging to her hair and clothes before they disappeared, taking Carol with them.

"Carol?" Dina rushed forward and turned in a slow circle, scanning for her friend, but Carol was nowhere to be seen. Looking back toward the door, Dina saw that it had disappeared as well.

Dina was alone in the forest. She picked up a single dry leaf and studied it carefully.

The leaf was brittle, barely holding together in the gentle fall breeze. Dina held it by the stem, watching as small pieces cracked apart and fluttered toward the leaf-strewn ground.

As the breeze blew and the sun warmed her face, Dina felt pieces of her thoughts fluttering away. Soon her mind would be completely clear.

§

Pumpkin Spice - Ep. 39, October 19, 2021

Fall is my favorite time of year. Sweaters, crisp air, and the brilliant display of changing leaves. Of course, it also brings the trend of pumpkin spice everything, including this writing prompt. I felt my way through this story and had no idea how it would end until Carol disappeared, showing me a way to bring it back to the opening paragraph.

Storage War

Frank stood frozen in the front hall. There was a key ring in his hand and an indignant frown on his face. The set of his shoulders said he wasn't going to back down, but the shifting of his feet betrayed his conflicted conscience.

Sybil stood in front of him, hands on her hips and lips pursed in an angry white line. A folded sheet of paper stuck out from one clenched fist, and her body blocked the front door. Jeanine hovered in the kitchen doorway, wringing her hands and biting her lip.

"You weren't even going to tell me," Sybil accused heatedly.

The flash in her eyes could have sparked on the steel of Frank's defense.

"I'd've told you," he shot back, curling the key ring into his meaty palm.

"Oh, sure," Sybil scoffed. "After you had your pick?"

"Let's calm down," Jeanine interjected with a timid step into the hall.

"I have a right to be angry!" Sybil threw her hands in the air. "My dear brother finds out Uncle Nate had a storage unit and instead of telling me so we could split it fairly—like the will says—he decides to creep off and check it out for himself. Typical."

"Typical?" Frank sputtered. "Typical? Name one time I've ever done a single thing to speak up for myself and my rights in this family."

"Your rights?" Sybil screeched, and Jeanine was quickly by her side, wrapping her shoulders in a consoling arm and quieting her with soft shushes.

"Take a breath, babe," she murmured, running a hand up Sybil's arm and turning to Frank with hopeful eyes. "Can we try to talk this out? Calmly?"

Frank ran his fingers through his hair, the key ring still dangling from one hand. He turned in a small circle and exhaled loudly before turning back to his sister and her wife.

"I took care of Uncle Nate for the last six years," he began slowly, laying out a case he'd stated before. "I brought him meals and drove him to the store. By the end, I was even helping him dress and clean up whenever the nurse wasn't here. He wanted me to have this house. He told me. Several times."

"That's not what it says in his will," Sybil returned primly. "Besides, I helped him pay for this house for the last 10 years. Money for repairs, for basic upkeep, and even for that new roof. Plus, I paid for that nurse."

"Well, if I had the money…"

"Don't start that!" Sybil cut Frank off with an angry stamp. "I will not feel bad about my financial success."

"I don't want you to feel bad," Frank spoke through gritted teeth. "I'm just saying, there's more than one way to help a person, and I gave up everything for Uncle Nate. Nights, weekends. If I'd taken that vacation with Diane instead of staying to help here, we might still be together…"

"Okay, this isn't helping." Jeanine stepped away from Sybil and moved into the space between the siblings, a place she'd been occupying most of the weekend.

"Let's not rehash all that," she continued with a sigh. "What's going on with this storage unit?"

"I found the bill for it!" Sybil waved the folded paper in the air. "Then caught him sneaking out with the keys."

She turned her attention to Frank with a sneer, "And I was coming in to see what you wanted for lunch."

Frank flushed and gritted his teeth. "I wasn't sneaking out with the keys…"

"You were!" Sybil cut in. "You are! Those are the keys in your hand, and you're headed for the front door!"

She crossed her arms over her chest and tossed her head scornfully.

"It's not a crime to be in the front hall!" Frank shouted back. "You don't know that I was going anywhere."

"Then why did you say that before about how Uncle Nate wanted you to have the house?"

"He did want me to have the house," Frank sighed with a shake of his head, but Sybil knew she had him.

"You brought that up because you were on your way to get whatever's in that storage unit and keep it for yourself. Because you think you're owed more than me. Because you're jealous of my success…"

"Sybil." Jeanine's voice held a warning. "Let's not go there."

"We're always there!" Sybil countered as tears of frustration gathered in the corner of her eyes. "They all expect me to just write a check for anything this family needs. They act like everything I have was just handed to me when I worked damn hard for it. You know I worked for everything I have!"

"I know, I know," Jeanine rubbed Sybil's arm and kissed her temple lightly.

Frank dropped his head to stare at his boots and mumbled, "I work hard, too."

The hall was silent except for Sybil's soft sniffling. Frank looked at the key ring and sighed.

"Get your shoes and coats," he told them gruffly. "Let's see what we're even fighting about."

They were quiet on the short drive to the storage unit. Frank's hands gripped the wheel and Sybil watched the trees pass by with wide eyes. In the backseat, Jeanine rubbed the back of her neck and hoped they could get through this day without another screaming match.

When they reached Uncle Nate's storage unit, Frank offered Sybil the keys, but she gestured for him to open the metal door. They were alone in one of the buildings interior hallways with nothing but a series of doors to break up the stark white walls. Jeanine held Sybil's hand as Frank unlocked the metal door and rolled it open.

They stood in the hallway, looking through the open door at two rows of metal shelves stacked with boxes of various electronics and appliances. From the hall, Sybil could see a computer, a microwave, a bread maker, a blender, an air fryer, a record player, a DVD player, and a printer.

"Did Uncle Nate have a… side business?" she asked uncertainly.

"He was 92," Frank replied with a roll of his eyes. "But there's the e-reader I bought him last Christmas."

"And the crock pot we gave him a few years ago," Jeanine added. "Are these gifts he didn't want?"

"We bought him that TV about five years ago," Sybil said thoughtfully, "and we paid to have someone install it."

"But he put it here instead?" Frank frowned, thinking of the crappy TV he'd been watching while this one gathered dust.

"Well, I guess we can take back the gifts we each gave him…" Sybil began, but Frank didn't let her finish.

"Oh, no. This is Uncle Nate's stuff, no matter who gave it to him, and the will says we're supposed to split it 50-50."

"Oh, sure, just take the gifts I gave Uncle Nate. Why not? I'm made of money, right?"

They were so busy arguing, neither Frank nor Sybil saw Jeanine slip into the storage unit and start examining the boxes.

"Uh, guys…" she interrupted after several minutes.

"What?" Sybil snapped, expecting another call for them to calm down.

"They're empty," Jeanine said simply.

"What?" Frank asked, pushing past his Sybil to check the boxes himself.

"Empty," Jeanine confirmed. "I guess he was just saving the boxes?"

"Why would he…?"

Sybil pushed her way into the unit and grabbed the nearest box. Jeanine stepped into the hall and watched as Frank and Sybil tore open each box and shook their heads at molded Styrofoam and plastic wrappings.

"They're empty," Sybil confirmed from her seat on the cement floor.

She looked at Frank and saw he was laughing.

"Do you want your half? Or should I take them all to the dumpster myself?"

Sybil looked at Jeanine, who had a hand over her shocked smile, and began to laugh herself.

"I'll help you," Sybil told her brother, accepting the hand he offered to help her up. "It's my inheritance, too."

§

Storage War - Ep. 44, November 30, 2021

Family is complicated, especially around the big events like weddings and funerals. I assume arguments over inherited storage units are fairly common, but I might enjoy the weirdness of inheriting one filled with empty boxes.

A New Leaf

The Empress had no need of a tracker. She deftly inspected the clearing herself, turning over leaves and sifting pebbles through her weathered hand. Someone had camped in the shade of the largest elm, though they'd taken care to scatter the remains of their small cooking fire and cover the depression from their night of rest with a smattering of leaves and brambles.

If the camp hadn't been obscured, the Empress may have doubted the identity of the traveler. As it was, she felt certain they were narrowing in on the woodcutter's trail.

"Will we camp here?" Jasper shifted his feet in the dry leaves and ran a hand beneath his dripping nose. The party was tired after their long ride, and he hoped to give them a rest before the sun fully rose.

Melinda stepped toward him, stroking Banyu's feathered back to calm the falcon against her strident tone.

"You would make camp?" she sneered. "With the woodcutter still free?"

"We've ridden for hours," Jasper returned weakly. "The horses…"

"The horses are well trained for hard service," Melinda rejoined. "It's a pity their master is not."

Jasper's face flushed as he straightened his stocky frame. The falconer towered over him, both in height and in her position as the Empress' right hand. It had only been a fortnight since they'd lost their Master of Horse and Hunt to the gryphons and Jasper had not stepped into his place easily.

"Enough," the Empress said firmly from her crouch near the elm.

Dusting her hands, she stood and returned to the eight-man hunting party. They'd taken the opportunity to dismount, pat down their tired steeds, and offer water around. Her lady in waiting held the reins of both their horses in one hand and a short sword in the other. Geneviève was always ready for whatever may come.

"The woodcutter is close and now travels on foot."

The party received the Empress' news with subdued cheer. Only Jasper's face broke into a wide grin as he clasped his hands in hope.

"On foot, is he? That's a break! And you're sure then?"

"You fool!" Geneviève rushed to his side, sword at the ready. "You doubt our lady's skill?"

The horses shuffled aside, and Jasper's face paled in shame.

"What? No! Of course, I wouldn't… Your highness, I didn't mean…"

The Empress waved away his words, turning to Geneviève with an indulgent sigh. "Let's allow a period of learning and remember the enemy we seek."

"Yes, ma'am," Geneviève agreed with a smirk that was understood to hold no disrespect.

The Empress gestured for Melinda's approach and spoke to her quietly. The other hunters gazed into the woods, on alert for signs of movement despite their relaxed appearance. Jasper began to tremble, and Geneviève took reluctant pity on him.

"You'll learn," she said sharply, adding a nod that he chose to accept as encouragement.

There had been very little encouragement—or reassurance of any kind—since he'd been rousted from bed and told he would be stepping in as interim Master of Horse and Hunt, until a replacement was chosen from among the elder huntsmen Though Jasper had been well suited as chief stableman, he did not feel prepared to take part in the hunt, let alone lead in this ceremonial fashion.

Jasper watched as the Empress stepped back and Melinda removed the falcon's leather hood. Banyu stretched his grey wings, and Jasper could swear he saw a red glow in the bird's sharp eyes. A moment later, Banyu took to the sky. Melinda closed her eyes and pressed her palms together in front of her heart.

The rest of the hunters took to their horses, though Geneviève maintained her guard on foot, keeping within easy reach of both the falconer and Empress. Jasper looked between the trio and the horsemen, unsure of his position. Stephen, a grizzled old hunter gave a quick tilt of his head, indicating Jasper's place among them, and Jasper hurriedly mounted his horse.

He'd no sooner settled his seat when Melinda yelled, "There!"

Her arm was outstretched, pointing toward a break in the trees. Her eyes shone red, just as Jasper had seen in the falcon.

"At the edge of a stream," she continued urgently. "Go!"

The horsemen surged forward, and Jasper followed, holding back the fear that he should be leading the pack instead of bringing up the rear. By the time Jasper reached the stream, Stephen had bound the woodcutter's wrists and was preparing to hoist him up for their return.

Back in the clearing, Jasper kept his distance as the woodcutter was dropped at the Empress' boots.

"Your Highness, please," the bedraggled man croaked as he struggled to his feet. "Have pity on a poor, misguided wretch."

"You allowed thieves into my larder," the Empress replied, ignoring his words to present him with his crimes. "You intended to profit from the sale of my goods—goods stored for all of my people—and two of my guards were killed in the thieves' attempted escape."

"They misled me," the woodcutter cried, dropping to his knees. "They promised no one would be harmed, and I wanted to provide my family with nice things."

"Nicer things than those I provide?" the Empress asked archly.

"No, no, I didn't mean—" The woodcutter stammered to a halt.

"You wanted to provide for your family," the Empress repeated thoughtfully. The woodcutter raised his hopeful gaze, nodding enthusiastically.

"Yes, yes. I was misguided but had only the best intentions! If you take pity on me now, I will never make such a mistake again. I'll begin again and change. I'll turn over a new leaf."

"Yes," the Empress agreed gravely. "You will."

Turning her back, she nodded once, and Melinda stepped forward. Jasper saw the other horsemen look down at their hands, but he couldn't bear to miss what would happen next. He stood a few paces behind Geneviève, watching with her as Melinda and Banyu turned their joined focus on the woodcutter.

Their eyes shifted from red to green and, in a flash, the woodcutter was gone. In his place stood a sturdy sapling with thin branches and pale leaves that swayed in a passing breeze.

Without looking back, the Empress addressed the party, saying, "He shall provide for his family and for all our people, adding shade to our forest and one day contributing to our stockpiles of wood, just as he did in life."

The horsemen nodded grave acceptance of her wisdom, turned their mounts, and waited as the Empress, Melinda, and Geneviève prepared to return to the castle. Jasper met the eyes of the Empress, who smiled kindly.

"You are learning," she told him, echoing the encouragement of her lady in waiting. "Once our true Master of Horse and Hunt is chosen, you may join their ranks and continue to grow in your new role."

Jasper thanked her humbly, and they rode back to the castle together.

§

A New Leaf - Ep. 47, December 28, 2021

Some free-written stories flow more easily than others. This one poured out as soon as I began describing the hunting party, reminding me that practice makes it easier to trust my creative instincts. Another benefit of regularly making time for free-writing.

Until Next Time...

Try a little free-writing of your own.
Let go of any planning and see where
your imagination takes you!

§

Find *Freely Written* on your favorite podcast app.

About the Author

Susan Quilty is an indie author who loves sharing her imaginary worlds through novels written for both adult and young adult readers. Her stories are grounded in reality yet often feature science fiction, fantasy, or psychological twists.

You can learn more about Susan and her upcoming projects by following her on social media or visiting her website: SusanQuilty.com.

Also by Susan Quilty

The Insistence of Memory - Reality bends when Joanne discovers her husband's secret creation: a machine that can record memories and play them back in someone else's mind. She must now decide whether to continue the project or protect the dark secrets in her own past.

To the Left of Death - When a teacher witnesses murder, she's unable to make peace with the experience. Will a return to her love of drawing revive her or pull her back into the mystery of that fateful day?

The Psychic Traveler Society Series - Fourteen-year-old Amanda Jones doesn't know that the Victorian house in her daydreams is about to lead her into worlds beyond her imagination. The series begins with *Healers and Thieves.*

Audrey and Esther Geekify Greenville - Choices in this "twist your fiction" book could add a sci-fi, fantasy, or rom-com twist to your adventure. With 22 possible endings, this book can be read again and again.